FIGHTING FOR HIS MATE

A SCI-FI ALIEN ROMANCE

FATED MATES OF THE ATARI
BOOK 3

A.G. WILDE

PETRONIE PUBLISHING

FIGHTING FOR HIS MATE

I don't want a mate.
Everyone knows this, so the fates should too.
When I'm thrown into a series of events that put me face to face with a human female, I know the fates must be playing a joke on me. When I end up fighting for the female, risking my life just so she will be safe, I start to get suspicious.

And when one smile from her makes my insides turn to floosh...I know something has gone wrong in the cosmos.
I'm not made for a mate...so why is my body telling me that I've found the female that thrums my heart string? And why does the thought of her being touched by someone else make me want to end every male in my path?

1

Mona

These aliens are scum.

How do I know? I used to live scum. Breathe scum. Take up scum, and destroy scum. I know what scum feels like. What it smells like. And certainly what it looks like. And these dark-green aliens before me look just like the type of shit I used to get paid to clean up.

That was my job back on Lower Earth. Traveling the streets in those big cleaner trucks. The same type of truck that took my left leg when I fell and the blades rolled over me.

Pity I don't have one of those trucks to roll over these assholes in front of me now.

Nothing about their outward appearance labels them as filth. If anything, their smooth dark-green skin almost shines in the stark white light that fills the ship. They decorate themselves with hanging jewels rather than clothing. Pretty reds, greens, and purples that shimmer and slide across their smooth skin as they totter around the ship.

But I see it in their eyes. The way they look at me.

The little, shifty black beads embedded into their skulls like the jewels they wear, dart my way and brighten even when I glare.

I am *nothing* to them.

Nothing more than a few credits.

Maybe they don't realize I can understand Galactic Standard. After all, they haven't tried conversing with me.

Not after they'd procured me from that murderer that took down the ship I was on. Not when they dragged me into this vessel and secured me to a pole in a corner of the bridge. And not while they discussed my future.

"The king awaits. We must make haste," one of them says, bustling in.

They are short. Squat. Probably reaching my belly button if I stand up straight.

I could *so* kick their asses if my hands were free. And that's probably why they'd drugged me the moment they'd bought me from that murderer.

The same murderer that killed every single woman that had gone on that "luxury cruise" I'd found myself a part of. An initiative of the New Earth government, it was supposed to herald a new life.

And I'd expected one. A new chapter out of the hell that was the Lower Levels of New Earth. A new beginning.

Just not *this* one.

But as time passes and I sit here on the floor, it's clear these aliens underestimated something. The drugs are wearing off and my mind is clearing. With every minute that goes by, I regain strength in my limbs. Lying here on the floor, my hands behind my back at the point where they'd secured me to the pole, I am unmoving, my lids lowered as I…wait.

Because I'm getting out of this.

Patience has never been my virtue, but it's going to be now.

To the aliens, I must look helpless. Woozy. Weak.

They're going to make a mistake—heck, they've already made a mistake with the dosage of this drug—and as soon as I get a chance, I am getting the hell out of here.

"The new games begin in one revolution. We will arrive on time," another of the aliens says.

Games?

They've used that word before, and each time they say it, an uneasy feeling goes down my spine.

What games? I sure as hell know they're not talking about checkers. And if I've learned anything since my existence began, it's that this universe is a cruel, cruel place.

One of the aliens glances my way, his eyes shifting over my form and a rumble goes through him as he shivers with glee.

"The specimen is perfect," he says.

Perfect?

Another word that makes unease go down my spine.

Where I come from, nobody is perfect. We are all *imperfect*. Especially me.

My flaws are outward. Obvious. And they characterize my body. My soul.

"Seeing the specimen within the ring will bring much pleasure to our king," another says. "Its death will be glorious."

I stiffen at those words, almost blowing my cover.

So wherever they're taking me, I'm bound to die.

Ha.

Well.

That makes things a helluva lot easier. A girl like me has nothing to lose if the end game is death anyway.

"We are in position," the alien's comrade says. "Activating hyper speed to our Darzel home world."

What had been a slight, constant hum in the depths of the ship increases enough that I fight to remain limp.

It almost feels like the cells deep inside me vibrate as the ship suddenly lurches forward, my body moving slightly, rising into the air and being thrust forward before everything snaps back into place.

"Broadcast the game," one of my captors says. "I wish to view this revolution's tournament."

The others rumble and chitter together with glee. There are three of them and they stand together before me, their backs turned my way as a holo image lights up the air in front of them.

At first, I can't make out what they're looking at and I have to squeeze my eyes shut tight, fighting off the sudden ringing in my ears followed by the churning in my gut. Side effects of traveling so fast, I presume. I might not be able to feel it now, but my body doesn't like it one bit.

Groaning, I shift, squinting as I point my gaze at the holo image.

I might as well try to figure out what type of "games" they intend for me to partake in when we arrive on their home world.

Prepare myself somehow…

But when my eyes land on the projected image, they fly open completely.

There, on the screen, are hundreds, no, thousands of aliens that look just like the ones before me.

They sit in a circular ring. Like the monumental structures built on Old Earth. Colosseums they used to call them. They shout and cheer, waving their arms, their faces filled with unhidden excitement.

The image pans to a section that looks different from the rest of the circle. A dais with an alien that looks exactly like the others except he's probably three times their size.

The king, I presume.

Hmm. I watch as there's more cheering. The crowd looks almost frenzied. What kind of game—

The thought dies in my head as the screen pans to the center of the arena and my whole body freezes.

At first, I'm not sure what I'm looking at. All I can see is a discolored section on the ground, the dirt stained by some kind of liquid, and when something darts across the screen, it all starts to make sense.

There's an alien running, utter terror on his face as he glances behind him. He's humanoid, like I am, except he's hairless, his skin a soft shade of blue. And that same skin is covered in streaks of green that look like his…blood.

I sit upright a little, my heart slamming into my chest as my eyes widen when something else appears on the screen.

It looks like those animals that used to roam Old Earth when there were forests. We got taught about them on National History days back when I was a child in standard education. Warthogs. Wild hogs? I can't remember the exact name. Those things don't exist anymore, so to see one now…

But it isn't exactly a warthog. The texts didn't describe them as being bigger than humans. And that thing on the screen…either the alien running for his life is smaller than I think…or that creature is over twenty feet tall.

Fuck.

I'm not scared of blood. Heck, when my leg got sawed off I didn't even faint. But as the creature catches the little blue alien and pierces him with a sharp tusk, blood splashes on the screen, covering it completely, and my insides curdle.

The aliens before me erupt in a collective shout, and I fight the urge to throw up.

These "games" they're talking about… It's nothing but murder. And this is what they're going to do to me?

Deep inside, where my heart should be, I feel an ache.

It's sharp, almost paralyzing, as my eyes shift to where my leg once was.

I can't run.

If they put me in that ring…I'm as good as dead.

As the screen clicks off, a plan hatches in my mind.

I have to kill them and get off this ship. But first, I have to get them to release these restraints.

What better way to achieve this than to fake my death? They can't bring me to those "games" if I'm already dead.

And so…for the first time in my life, I swallow my heart and my fear, and I put on a show.

As the aliens turn around, I arrest myself, shaking my body as if I'm having a seizure.

Saliva froths in my mouth as I up the ante.

This is the performance of, quite literally, my life. And when alarm rings in those beady black eyes as they turn and see me flopping on the floor, I know I've got them in the palm of my hand.

2

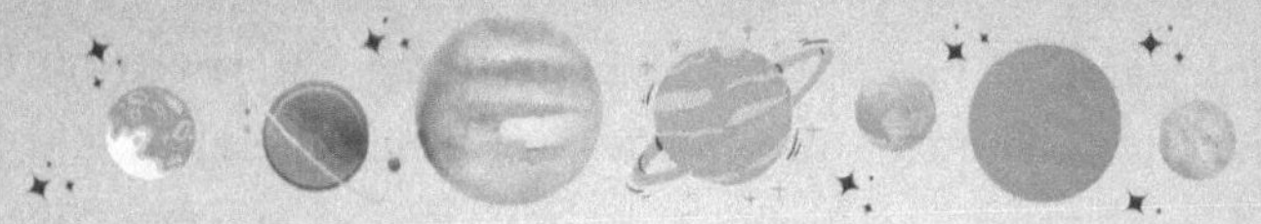

Bhihan

I never thought I enjoyed the company of my brothers. But now that I am alone in the Zarzenius, the boredom is driving me crazy.

All three of the males I travel with have gone seeking possible survivors of the massacre that took away the potential bridal gift given to us by New Earth.

Precious females. Some of them no doubt mates for my Atari kin.

Sitting on the swivel chair at the center of the bridge, I pull up schematics across the viewscreen.

For more than one rotation, I have been trying to get in contact with Qhenno. Helmsman of this ship, he shouldn't have gone after the lead we got concerning one of the lost females. But he did. And to the Morang's mines.

That's a place no one ever escapes from. He was insane to go.

Sending a communication request to his shuttle, I swivel in the chair, my head falling back in boredom as I wait. Like all the other times, I expect the signal to return unanswered. So when the line connects, I almost fall from my seat.

"Qhenno?" I hop from the seat, surprised and somewhat annoyed at the anticipation flooding through me. For many moons, I have lived life without family. Without a mate. The companionship of these men I travel with has been all I needed. And that is even clearer now from my response to simply hearing my brother's voice once more.

For that fact, I clear my throat, frowning at myself as I reign in those emotions that have suddenly gone astray.

"Qhenno, if you can hear this, you need to contact the Zarzenius immediately."

There's no response for a few moments and I lean forward in the chair, straining my ears to pick up anything across the line.

If Qhenno is in trouble… if his shuttle was hijacked…

But even as these worrisome thoughts travel across my mind, I hear his hoarse voice. "I'm here."

"You qeffer." Annoyance fills me immediately. Why was I even worried? "Standard protocol is to send updates back to the Zarzenius. You went silent. I thought the Morang had imprisoned you in one of their mines."

"Oh, Bhihan," the qeffer growls, "I knew you loved me."

That's it. I'm never again becoming concerned about these so-called brothers of mine. There's a reason I keep a tight leash on my emotions. This is one of them.

"Save such words for the mate you want so badly," I return his growl. "Did you find the human?"

"I have her here. We will arrive at the Zarzenius shortly. We are about to go hyper-speed…and then you can have the pleasure of meeting my mate."

Qhenno's words make something within me falter and the utter pride in his voice makes that same thing ache.

A mate?

"Your *what*?" Is all I can say. Words fail me.

A mate? So, he too has found his fated.

Who would have thought? First Aqnar, the Zarzenius' second in command, and now Qhenno. Da'red, the captain of our ship and crown prince of Atar, is bound to find a mate as well. He is royalty, after all.

So…where does that leave me?

A mate is not in my future. I am not seeking one, nor are the fates willing to bestow one on me. And I can't help but think that this, for me, is the end.

With three of the four of us mated, our crew will dissolve. Mated males don't go on missions that endanger their lives. They have more than simply fighting for Atar to keep them going.

They have females to live for.

There is no greater purpose.

Hearing Qhenno's proclamation only means one thing...

I'll have to find another crew to travel with.

"Speak to you soon, Bhihan..." Qhenno says, and I am brought back to the present, focusing on the view screen before me.

Like a star going down across the horizon, the sense that a chapter of my existence is ending weighs down on my conscience like a dark cloud.

One that suddenly bursts with light as something erupts right in front of the Zarzenius.

"Gods of Atar!" I press down on the control panel, eyes wide as my life organ slams into my chest. "What in the qef?!"

In the background, I hear Qhenno, but I can't pull my gaze away from the sight before me.

"I told you that I was drawn to the mines..." Qhenno begins.

"No, not you. There's a transport that just jumped from hyper-speed right in front of the Zarzenius."

"Isn't that dangerous?" I hear his mate whisper, and another pang goes through that space in my chest.

That's something I have to deal with later. I have already accepted my fate...and I don't want a mate. There is no reason for me to feel this way.

Leaning toward the viewscreen, my brows lift.

There's movement on the side of the transport and I squint, using the view screen to zoom in so I can take a closer look.

"By the gods..." I whisper. "There's a being..." I activate the zoom to two hundred percent, my eyes widening some more. "A *female*?"

What in the qef?

There, on the side of the transport, the female clutches on to the support ladder that runs up the side of the vessel. Dressed in gear that protects her from the void, I only know it's a female because she turns and looks directly at the Zarzenius.

Determined eyes meet mine in the camera and I freeze, a part of me turning to ice as I stare at her.

She's trying to make her way to the back of the transport where the escape pods are. Why not take the corridor *inside* the ship? Only an insane person—

When I spot movement behind her, a Darzel lifting his weapon and shooting in her direction, missing her by mere inches, I get my answer.

A growl rumbles in my chest the moment I spot the scum.

The Darzel are a species that colonized their planet, eradicating every other half-intelligent species on their world. They're well-known for their thirst for blood and entertainment, often combining the two, and it's no secret they traffic intelligent beings from lesser planets, forcing them to perform in their cruel games.

It all comes into place in a matter of seconds.

The female…she's fighting for her life.

In the background, Qhenno's directing me to hail the female. To tell her to veer off-course. But as I head from the bridge, I already know. There isn't anyone flying that ship.

I must have said it out loud because Qhenno's shouting even more commands. But I can only focus on one thing now.

Activating the Zarzenius' artificial intelligence, I head to the flight deck as I strap on my jetpack and pull on my suit.

If she's running from the Darzel, it means she's not one of them. And if she's not one of them, they have captured her. They're not the type to make friends with other species.

I have to help her.

I should have picked it up sooner. She's too tall. Too lithe. Darzel are much shorter. But what they lack for in size they make up for with the poison glands all across their skin.

"Wait, Bhihan—"

I know what my brother is about to say. That I should divert the Zarzenius. But our ship is big and moving it in time requires one of two things. I can either go to hyper speed, which will kill the female and every other being on the transport approaching, or I can turn the Zarzenius so the eventual collision doesn't harm our ship.

In both cases, the female will die.

But there is a third option. I can save her.

Qef me.

As I jump off the flight deck, the void swallowing me as I activate the jetpack strapped to my back, I wonder if I am just as insane as my brothers.

3

Mona

I scream into the helmet encasing my head as something hot sears my leg.

"Fuck!"

The bastard chasing me shot me.

Grimacing, I keep on moving, hanging on for dear life as I head toward the back of the ship.

"Fuck fuck fuck fuck *fuck*!"

Right in front of us, there's a huge ass ship. The biggest I have ever seen in my life, and I wonder if they are friend or foe. But there's no time to think about that. I have to get my ass into the escape pod nestled at the back of this cursed transport ship. But even as I move, I feel the wound freezing over. My skin's exposed to the void.

Knowing this, my heart almost falters.

No.

No no no no no.

I can't die like this.

Alarms blare in the suit I basically dragged on as I glance behind me to see the annoying little fucker still giving chase.

"The fuck?!"

He's not wearing a suit. Instead, there's this thick layer of goo that's all around his body. It freezes and falls away as he climbs after me, only to regenerate just as fast.

I curse at him as I turn and try to move faster. But that little hole in my suit is causing my leg to freeze, even as the suit tries to battle the loss of pressure and maintain temperature controls.

At this rate, I won't make it. My goose is cooked.

But I *have* to get to that escape pod.

Thank fucking God I learned to read Galactic Standard. All those shit people threw away that I had to clean up, some of them were priceless. Like information cards that were like encyclopedias. I used to devour them whenever I had the chance.

It's the only reason I was able to read the layout of this ship and figure out where the escape pods were. The only reason I found this suit, lucky they made it with stretchy material that could fit over my long limbs.

After my little acting gig to save my life, the idiots removed the restraints to "revive" me. "A loss," they'd said. "Death too easy," they'd chided.

I'd taken the first opportunity as soon as it presented itself. My boot found its way into one of their heads as I rolled and grabbed the same boot, pulling it off my foot and using the hard heel to clobber the other.

I must be stronger than I think, because those two went down easily.

Only one left, I'd thought. *Shouldn't be too hard after all.*

But you know those famous last words you snicker at when watching holo vids? Yep. I'd been wrong.

As the one that was left raced down the corridor, I heard him screaming for backup. Rising on my leg, I hopped forward to see another four of the bastards racing down the corridor toward me, with the one that had run to call them diverting to grab a blaster.

I'd headed through the closest door and locked myself in. I had to continue moving.

I worked with machines that chewed up scum, but every machine

I've worked with had artificial intelligence. I'd used that knowledge, asking the ship to show me where the escape pods were.

There was no way I could retrace my steps based on the diagram it showed me. It was either go through the maintenance hatch…or open the door and face five very livid aliens.

And now, here I am—crawling *outside* the ship, fire in my leg as I swing like a monkey, using only my arms to carry me across the rungs that lead to the back of the ship.

The alarms in the suit continue to blare. Energy being used to keep the rest of my body warm while that one spot in my leg feels like it's being burned by a hot rung.

I have to make it.

Otherwise…

I don't even want to think about it. But when another blast shoots through space right beside my head, my heart seizes.

Shit.

Glancing behind me once more, I wish I could kick the fucker off and as I bite my bottom lip, the urge to see him fall into the void is almost so strong, I can feel it in my bones. I may have also prayed a little.

Prayed for him to slip on that goo he's using to protect himself, or for some god to save me.

That's when I see the thing approaching.

And I say *thing* because, at first, I don't know what the hell I'm looking at.

Something gold, glinting in the light that's reflected on its exterior, is heading this way. No doubt it's coming from the direction of that huge golden ship that we'll crash into at any moment.

A missile?

No. It's not moving fast enough.

And…it has arms. I see them now and realize just how fast the thing is moving.

A man?

Those arms grab the side of the ship I'm holding on to and I pause, frozen in shock, as I watch the newcomer use his boot in much the same way that I did before.

With one well-aimed kick, his boot connects with the scum that's chasing me. Stunned, the alien releases his hold on the ship, his eyes widening as he falls. Arms flailing, desperate to regain his hold.

In another circumstance, I might have felt sorry for him. But my heart's gone stone cold.

Eyes darting back to the newcomer, my brows rise. Maybe my prayers have been answered.

God?

I almost mouth the words out of pure delirium, but when harsh golden eyes find me, looking right into my soul from the transparent face of his helmet, I know I'm wrong.

God wouldn't glare at me like that.

It *is* a man. An incredibly handsome one from what I can see, and he's currently shouting something unintelligible as he makes his way toward me, shooting through the air using some device strapped on his back.

He shouts some more and I wonder if he's an idiot.

Of course, I can't hear him. I can't hear shit in this suit.

He snarls at me so hard I see a set of pure white fangs before he points behind him.

My eyes widen when I get what he's saying.

That huge ship is getting closer and unless someone does something, we're going to crash right into it.

I glare back at him.

"I know, you fool! That's why I'm trying to get the hell out of here!"

Those liquid gold eyes of his go blank, just before one side of his brows lift, almost as if he can't believe I'm shouting back at him. Now he's looking at me as if I'm insane.

Before I can react, his huge arm snakes around my waist.

Nope.

I wriggle in his grasp, forcing my leg to move as I kick, pushing myself forward and pulling him with me.

He's shouting again and I only know because I look back in time to see some short phrases leave his lips. He's cursing. Ah well.

"Let me go!"

I'm almost at the damn escape pod and that's where I'm going to go. I'm sure I can get to safety from there.

This dude might seem like he's trying to help me, but I've had enough of extraterrestrials since embarking on that so-called luxury cruise.

Aliens can't be trusted.

The only person I can trust is me. Mona McKnight.

As I force myself forward against the pull of this newcomer, I sense when he finally gives in and releases me.

Pushing forward, I think he's going to leave, but surprise fills me when he appears before me instead, using the jetpack at his back to go around me and directly to the hatch that leads to the entrance of the escape pods.

For a moment as he hovers there at the hatch, I wonder if he's about to do something that will thwart my plans. Fear trickles through me with every beat of my heart.

But he doesn't do anything nefarious.

Golden eyes on the ship that will be our doom, he opens the hatch and pierces me with his gaze.

I nod, moving forward and sliding into the dark hole.

There is no gravity control here with the hatch open, and I float, my eyes on the escape pods as my heart thunders in my chest.

I try to butterfly swim through the air toward them when gravity suddenly kicks in.

I land on my ass, pain shooting through my spine and my leg burning as if someone's put a heated brand through it.

Far in the bowels of the ship, I can hear the other green aliens shouting. I have to get to that escape pod and fast. Crawling upright, I brace on my leg and hop, my intent before me. But I'm suddenly barred by a huge golden frame.

Oh shit. He'd entered behind me? I thought he'd shut the hatch and gone about his business.

More shouting in the bowels of the ship, getting louder. I have to get out of here now.

"You're in my way." I try to go around him, but the newcomer grabs me by the arm, causing me to lose my balance.

Reaching out, I grab the only thing there to hold on to. Him.

I swear I feel him grunt.

What is he doing?!

At the same time that I deactivate my visor, that clear screen that protects his face disappears.

"What the hell is your problem?!" We speak at the same time and both look at each other stunned.

His voice is deep, almost gruff, and catches me off guard.

"I'm trying to save you," he growls.

"I'm trying to save *myself!*"

Again, we stare at each other.

"Good gods," he finally says. "What did you say?"

"Let me go, this ship is going to blow and I need to get the hell out of here."

"And how are you planning to do that?"

I look at him stupidly. Who is this dude?

"The escape pod."

He turns with me still clinging on to him. *"That* escape pod?"

It only hits me then that he's speaking in Galactic Standard as I glance across his shoulder, my gaze landing on my sole escape.

The escape pod is a circular thing that looks like something only a child would fit in. It could probably work if I bend and fold myself, and that's exactly what I plan on doing.

"Yes," I state, trying to right myself, but the stranger won't let me go.

"You can't use that," he says, turning to stare down at me.

"Look, it's small, but it will fit. I don't really have a lot of time to make this decision."

He shakes his head, pointing to the pod. It's only then that I see a thin sheen of goo glistening on its surface.

"Ugh." My nose wrinkles. Those slimy motherfuckers.

"Toxic," he says. "Touch it and you'll be temporarily paralyzed."

Fuck.

My fingers are covered by the suit I'm wearing and for a moment, I wonder if it will work like a glove. I'm almost about to chance it when a hum goes through the ship. One I've heard before. My eyes widen as my fingers dig into the stranger's suit as I struggle to right myself.

"Hyper speed. They're going hyper speed again."

I'm balancing on my leg when the stranger releases me and races down the corridor.

In the fight before, the controls had somehow been disengaged and we'd fallen out of hyper speed. But now that they're going back online can only mean they're set on returning to their planet.

Shit.

That's the exact reason I've been trying to escape in the first place.

Glancing at the escape pod, I grit my teeth, my brows diving when I turn away from it and hop in the direction the stranger had gone.

This is a mistake. I should take my chances and try opening the escape pod.

So why am I heading in the stranger's direction?

I don't know how I get there so quickly, chest heaving as I brace on the door frame leading onto the bridge.

There, I see the stranger spin midair, sending a flying kick into the face of one of the green aliens.

I only see one other moving alien.

So, that's what, five he's possibly killed. Six? I can assume he's really on my side now, right? As another charges at him, body brimming with goo, he sidesteps and brings a metal pole down unto the fiend's head.

No idea where he got that weapon from, and I don't care, because when he locks eyes with me, those golden pits flare.

Just…who the hell is he?

Our gazes stay locked for just a few moments too long when I see movement in my periphery.

"Look out!"

But it's too late. The stranger snaps his eyes from mine just as a narrow pole of goo shoots through the air, hitting him straight in the face. With his visor up, it splashes right onto his skin.

He roars and attempts to chase after the green alien, just before his knees buckle, those golden eyes catching mine once more—only now filled with raging fires.

The pole he was using to beat the fuckers clangs to the ground as he grits his teeth, furious eyes locked with mine as he falls flat on his face.

Shit.

The green alien laughs and it's clear he doesn't realize I'm standing at the door.

As I swallow hard, my eyes on the stranger, hoping that he'll get back up, I know he won't move when the green alien walks over and stands on his back.

Is he dead?

My heart skips a beat.

But no. He can't be dead.

He'd said something about their goo being toxic. He's just paralyzed.

That means I'm the only one here to do something about that fiend who's standing on his back like he's just won a tournament.

My eyes fall on the metal pole the stranger had been using and I'm moving even before the thought solidifies.

Rolling onto the floor, I grab the pole with both hands, the momentum carrying me forward as I grip the weapon and swing upward.

I only see those beady eyes of the fiend as it lands on me, right before I slam the pole into his body.

He crumples, falling off the stranger, and I roll to my belly, slamming the pole into his gut, his head, his legs, anywhere it will land until he isn't moving anymore.

I'm out of breath by the time I try to rise into a sitting position.

There's no movement on the bridge and no other sound in the ship apart from the constant hum of the engine.

Bracing on the pole, I use it to stand.

They'd taken away my crutches long ago when those murderers killed everyone on that cruise and took me hostage. Bracing on the pole now, it's long enough that it will do.

Moving over to the control panel, my fingers hover over the controls. It's all written in some other language than Galactic Standard and a curse leaves my lips.

"AI?" I speak out loud. "Ship?"

"Greetings, Earthkin."

"How do I take the ship out of hyper speed?"

"Command denied. You do not hold the necessary clearance."

"Change destination."

"Command denied. You do not hold the necessary clearance."

"Fuck." I pause. "Where's this ship heading?"

"Destination: Darzel."

"Fuck that. If we're still on the trajectory for that horrible world I saw projected on the vid screen, I'll take my chances with the escape pod."

I'm starting to turn when the AI speaks again.

"No Darzel lifeforms detected. Protocol 129 activated. All escape devices disengaged. All exits locked. This vessel is returning to homeworld Darzel."

I freeze. "Say what now?"

"Protocol 129 activated. This vessel is returning to homeworld Darzel."

Eyes widening, I turn back to the control panel, panic making me hit the buttons there, not caring which one I hit or what it does.

Nothing happens.

"No. No no no no no."

Leaning on the control panel, I run my hands through my braids, my heart slamming against my chest as reality slowly sinks in.

"FUUUCK!"

Sliding to the floor, my head falls into my hands as I fight to control my breathing.

This is a death sentence.

I almost forget that I'm not alone when I hear a groan that makes my shoulders stiffen.

4

Bhihan

Qef me.

She's human. I'm sure of it.

And I'm also sure she's left me here for dead.

Frowning into the floor against my face, I wonder what the qef the female is doing and why she hasn't come to, at least, roll me over.

I'm an Atari warrior. I have dignity, even if it's just a little.

I'm surprised she managed to kill one of the Darzel. I expected her to run and hide. But what was even more surprising was her determination to get off this vessel.

Instead of batting even one eye at me, she left me in a puddle of spittle as she hobbled to the control panel. There, it's obvious she tries to turn this vessel around, with what's obviously no experience piloting craft like this.

But we are still alive, at least. Even a brute like me can thank the gods the Darzel were smart enough to turn the vessel before engaging hyper speed once more. Otherwise, we would have collided with the Zarzenius and turned to dust.

I release a groan, lucky my throat is still working. It comes out muffled, my lips unable to move, and I grunt into the floor, annoyed and uncomfortable.

I'm immobile and stuck on a Darzel craft. Away from my people, my ship, and my weapons. What's worse, no one will know where I've gone.

Qef!

I hear a string of curses the moment the ship's artificial intelligence tells the female the exact thoughts that are flying through my head. Hearing its words only makes me want to growl.

We are stuck. And it's all her fault.

If I could growl at her, I would. But then it hits me like a brick and I curse at myself for being so slow to realize.

If she's human, what is she doing out here on a Darzel ship? And… if she's human…what are the chances she's one of the females we've been searching for?

For a moment, I perk my ears, hoping to hear her movement somewhere behind me. As soon as this toxin wears off, I need to find out where she came from.

It would be too much of a coincidence for me to discover one of those humans so strangely. Too much like the fates meant it to be.

As soon as that thought surfaces in my head, I push it away.

The fates have never worked on my side. If they have put this female in my path, I can almost guarantee she will break me with strife.

So I focus on my anger instead. And I direct it at her.

If not for her, I could have been sitting on the bridge of the Zarzenius eating all the floosh I could ever want and not caring about anything. I could spend my boring days simply waiting for my brothers' return. And when I saw her hanging on the side of this vessel, destined to collide and die, I could have just let it be.

The worst that would happen to the Zarzenius is that the shield would be somewhat depleted. It's far too large to have suffered much from impact with this small craft.

Why the gods did I not keep my position on the Zarzenius and let this female come to her end?

I groan again, the sound moving up my throat in an awkward manner that makes my chest vibrate against the floor.

Anger. Focus on anger.

I do this, just to ignore that niggling feeling at the back of my mind. The one that tells me if time were reversed, I'd do the same thing all over again.

I'd still leave the Zarzenius and come after the female.

Everything I just said was a lie.

Because I am Atari. And every Atari knows that females are special. Even one who will never fall to the temptation of having one for his own.

I'm so lost in my thoughts that I don't realize the room has gone silent. So silent, I wonder whether the female has shuffled off somewhere without me realizing.

She has use of only one leg. I noticed the moment I arrived and helped her dispose of the captor chasing her. How she even evaded the Darzel and got on the outside of the ship is a story I'd love to hear. That is, if she wasn't now at the top of my list of people to avoid.

I'm still so consumed by annoyance that I almost miss the slight sniffle.

Wait.

What's that?

I try to turn my head in the direction of the sound but I am really and truly paralyzed.

I hear the sniffle again and something deep inside me folds in on itself.

The female...is she...feeling such sorrow that waters have come to her eyes?

I groan again.

I really am the worst sort of male.

While I'm here nurturing my anger towards the female, she is probably hiding in some corner behind me, completely hopeless and scared out of her wits.

Grunting again, I try to shift myself to no avail. But at the sound I make, I hear the female move.

Another word like a curse comes from her lips. One that would make me frown if my facial muscles were movable.

The steady hit of the end of the metal pole against the floor is what reaches my ears next until a leather boot appears before my eyes.

She crouches and I strain to see her face.

Poor little female. She must be so terrified.

When she tilts her head till I can see her face, I expect trembling lips and eye waters running over her dark skin.

Instead, what I see is a scowl.

She sniffles again and my eyes widen slightly.

She isn't sniffling because she is in tears. She's stifling for some other reason. And the look on her face isn't of a person that's scared out of their wits. It's of someone who is just as annoyed as I am.

Balancing on her leg, she pushes the metal pole into my side and grunts.

"This is your fault."

My eyes widen some more in the only defiant thing I can do.

This is certainly not my fault.

She pokes me again and I glare at her some more. Does this female have no sense of respect? I am on my face on the floor and—

She grunts again and uses the pole to support her as she stands.

She's going to leave me here? Again?

I growl, the sound rumbling through me and she pauses, uttering a sound like a "tsk" from her lips.

"Fine," she says.

The metal pole clangs to the floor so close to my head that my ears ring. When I wonder what other torture she will make me suffer, she falls to her knee before me.

Lifting my gaze, all I can see is the apex of her thighs and how the suit she's wearing snaps to her like a second skin. Pulling my eyes away from that sight takes more effort than it should, but I'm spared any embarrassment when the female grunts and pushes against my shoulder.

"Fuck me, you're big."

Huh?

My eyes fly to her again as she grunts and pushes against me. With much effort, she leans me on my side and I finally get a better view of her.

This close, I can even smell her.

And this incredibly ill-mannered, annoying female smells unnervingly...*delicious*. She's soft too. So very soft as she braces her chest and arms against me, trying to roll me over.

I'm staring at her as she assaults me, and the sensitive skin at the back of my neck pulses as if I am in danger, just as she grabs the metal pole and shoves it against my chest.

My eyes widen slightly as she pushes with all her might and I fall on my back with a thud. I am a bulky male. My body has more muscle than anything else.

What is there to do when you live most of your life on a ship floating in the void? As one of the crown prince's guards, I have trained long and hard to be a force enemies will quiver and flee from.

So when this female grunts and leans back on her arms, dark brown eyes on me, why is it that something quivers inside *me*? Why do *I* have the urge to run?

"Pity you're so handsome..." Her eyes narrow. "Annoying. Like pretty babies. The only reason you put up with their shit is because they're cute. Well," she braces on the floor and stands, "rolling you over is all the help you're getting from me. Call it even for you killing that dude that was chasing me on the outside."

I blink at her.

Did she...

Did she just compliment and insult me at the same time?

I growl at her and, in her impertinence, she rolls her eyes at me.

The fates must be laughing.

I change my mind. I should have left her to fend for herself and kept my ass on the Zerzenius.

I could be happy eating my floosh.

5

Mona

This surly idiot is glaring at me as if I killed his mother.

I ignore him as I move around the ship, accessing as many panels as I can and amassing a hoard in the center of the room.

So far I've found blasters, blankets, weird circular objects that I have no clue the purpose of, and things that look like tools.

I've also cleared the bridge of the dead vermin that were lying over various sections of the floor. They were a pain to drag and lock into one of the empty storage bays at the back. It was even harder taking care not to touch their skin, which seemed to be secreting even more goo now that they no longer breathed.

But I grunt and bear it, biding my time. There's a knot of nerves in the center of my chest. Anxiety and some fear about what comes next. I need to be prepared so that when we arrive at this new planet, I can defend myself.

Heck, maybe I can even tinker with this ship and get the AI to disregard its protocol.

All my adult life, I've worked with machines. I live, breathe, and sleep mechanics. Pity it was one of those same machines that took one of my greatest assets.

I'd always been proud of my long legs.

Back in the day, when New Earth was just called 'Earth', I could have probably been a model, walking runways and showing off garments that breathed elegance. Back then, when the world wasn't divided into levels and people like me didn't suffer because they weren't whole.

Shaking my head, I push the thoughts away as I open a storage panel to see an array of packets that can only be food.

Grabbing a few, I wince as I put too much pressure on my leg.

Turns out even my dark skin can't hide the universe's greatest hickey that's now on my thigh. A result of being kissed by space itself.

Cursing the alien that shot me and eroded the only protection I'd had against the void, I grab as many food packets as I can and return to the center of the room.

The white-haired alien stranger flicks his gaze to me immediately.

I wasn't lying when I said he was handsome.

His face is sculpted, his firm jaw complemented by a straight nose. He almost looks human, if not for the molten golden eyes and fangs that I can see peeking out from his slightly open lips. And his skin. Bronze and just as rich as the color in his eyes. Added to the white hair I see peeking from underneath his suit, he's striking.

I've never seen hair so pure white before. Each strand is like silky white thread spun by the finest weaver. He's ridiculously good-looking…and, he probably would be even more handsome if he wasn't still glaring at me.

I settle on the floor before him, eyeing him before shifting my eyes to the packets in my hand. They're written in some language other than Galactic Standard and I have no clue what's inside.

There are no images on the packaging either. Just blocks of unreadable text.

Chewing my bottom lip, I debate simply opening the things and trying a little bit of each. But I'm not keen on poisoning myself. Though, that might be an easier death than what is possibly in store for me when this craft reaches its destination.

"Can you read this?"

I swear his brows dip as he glares at me. It's more movement from him than a few minutes ago and that can only mean the toxin's effect is lessening. Reaching for the metal pole, I pull it towards me in case he tries something. But he only continues to glare at me.

Wincing again as I stretch my leg, I wave one of the packets at him.

But his eyes are now on my leg and, for some reason, I freeze. It's not like I'm not used to it. Whenever I had to travel to the Upper Levels to carry out some cleanup job they didn't want to do themselves, I always saw the looks. The humans that live up there look at people like me with a mixture of pity and a little curiosity.

And as I pause, I wait for those two things to appear in the eyes of the stranger before me.

Neither do.

His eyes flick back to mine and all I see is that same anger and annoyance.

The complete lack of the emotions I expected to see almost makes me chuckle. It's...nice not seeing that look in a stranger's eyes. So for now, I welcome his anger.

"Is it edible?" I shake the packet at him.

His eyes narrow, but other than that, there's no indication whether I can eat this thing. And I'm starving.

Months ago, or, at least, it feels like it was months ago, I left New Earth on a luxury space cruise organized by the government.

That trip had come to a quick end just one day into the cruise when the ship was overtaken by some beings that call themselves the Khuru.

They murdered everyone. I still don't know how or why they spared my life, but after that, everything was a blur.

They passed me around from Khuru to Khuru while they traveled to various markets. Each time I thought I was going to be sold, I wasn't. Not until these green beings, the Darzel, bought me off those murderers.

I'd hoped for a break. Hoped the nightmare had finally come to an end the moment I was bought. But deep down, I knew that was just wishful thinking.

Beings that bought from murderers were probably as evil as the murderers themselves.

Sighing, I bite the edge of the packet, ready to pull it open with my teeth, my gaze on the alien before me.

If it's poisonous, he makes no indication that it is.

Can't say he doesn't want me to die.

Maybe he hopes I eat it and fall unconscious.

Suspicious, my eyes narrow at him as I rip open the packet with my teeth. Whatever's inside squirts out like it was pushed with a jet, shooting right over my shoulder. I startle and yelp.

"Whoa." I glance over my shoulder to see a pink jelly on the floor. I can't tell if it's food or not.

There's a sound and when I look back at the stranger, there's now another clear emotion in his eyes.

Humor.

What's so funny?

Ok, so it seems I have to open this thing and let it shoot into my mouth?

Not gonna happen when I don't know what it is.

As soon as the idea hatches in my mind, I see the stranger's eyes widen slightly, his glare returning with an ounce of incredulity, as if he can read my mind.

I chuckle and without a word, I shuffle over to him, closing the distance between us.

His mouth is still slightly open and I can see the dangerous tip of one of those white fangs. Leaning toward him, he grunts, brows diving as I lift a second packet and bring it to his teeth.

He grunts again and I lock gazes with him just before I use his teeth to nick the packet. The pink jelly splooshes into his mouth.

He glares at me, but he doesn't look frantic. Guess he knows what this thing is after all.

As I bite into another packet and the jelly splooshes into my mouth, a sweet flavor bursts across my tongue. It tastes like a fruit blend and I finish the packet in just a few sips.

"This is actually good," I murmur and stranger dude narrows his eyes at me. Releasing a breath, I lean against him, throwing one arm back on his chest as I devour two or three more packets.

When I glance at him again, he's looking at me as if I am a strange being. I'm about to chuckle when his throat moves with so much effort, it's clear the muscles are still a bit frozen.

Eyes darting to the metal pole, I wonder if I should get it. If he's starting to move, shouldn't I be more careful?

But before I can move, words stop me in place.

"You have some nerve, female."

6

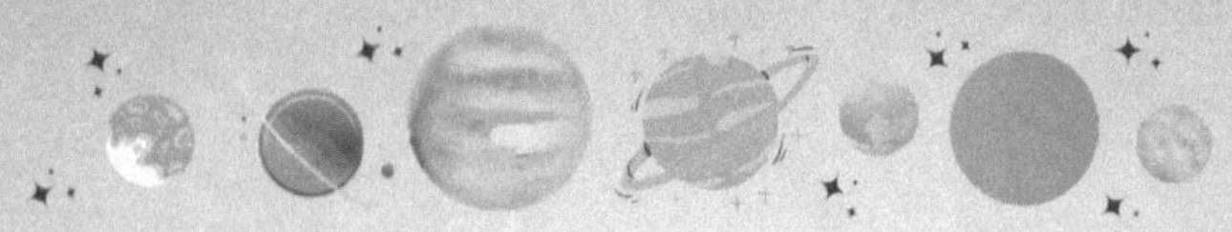

Bhihan

Fates, tell me, why is this female using me as a backrest? And after feeding me floosh she thought was poisonous?

As soon as I speak, her gaze darts at me and she freezes, shifting slightly toward the metal pole.

She doesn't trust me, yet she was leaning on me like it was nothing?

"You are a strange one."

"Says the man glaring at me for what feels like hours."

Mm, this delicious sound coming from her lips. Her voice is like thick nectar. Husky and soft at the same time. I almost feel it move across my skin. But her next words pull me from whatever tangent my mind was straying off on.

"It's your fault we're here, you know."

"What?" Did she really just blame me for this? "This is *your* fault. If you had just come with me—"

"Well, pardon me for not trusting you as soon as you arrived. Every alien I've met in the last few months has only been honorable, after all."

"I—" Hmm…she has a point. "I can tell you now, female. I mean you no harm. My brothers and I have been searching the cosmos for you, after all."

She stiffens again, her brows diving.

She has a small nose set over the plumpest lips that she twists as she stares at me, long braids swinging in the air as the spins to face me.

"Looking for me? You don't even know who I am."

I study her.

Pointed brown eyes look at me as if she is trying to see into my soul.

"You are human, are you not?"

She moves a little away from me, the warmth of her touch leaving with her.

"You left New Earth on a cruise with some other females."

Her eyes widen slightly, yet she gives no other sign I am on the right track.

"The Khuru overtook your ship. They…" I hesitate, unsure whether I should rehash the details of the massacre that occurred on that ship. Most females would not want to hear such things. I don't know of any Atari female—

"They killed them all. I was covered in the blood of my people, women just like me, for months. Reminded every second that it could have been me…and wondering why it hadn't been." Those eyes of hers meet mine and the fear and distress I expect to see within their depths is nowhere to be found. "Who…who are you? How do you know this? And why have you been looking for me?"

I study her some more, letting silence fall between us.

The anger I had been nurturing for her is suddenly gone, and for a moment, I frown, annoyed by that fact.

She is obviously smart. Intelligent. I can't trust this female who was willing to poison me while relaxing against my dying body as she ate my most favorite food in the universe. What are the chances of the Darzel having floosh on board? It's as if I was meant to come on board.

"I am Bhihan of Atar," is all I say and one of her eyebrows lifts.

"Well, Bhihan from Atar…why were you looking for me? And…

how did you just happen to be there, out in space, at the right possible time?"

That's my question too. Which god is playing a joke on me?

"The fates..." I begin, but not even I can answer her question with logic. Only the fates know why they sent her the moment she did. The Darzel ship shouldn't have exited hyper speed with a possible collision in front of it.

"You Earthkin made a trade with us Atari," I say instead. "A bridal gift in exchange for—"

"A what now?" Brown eyes widen. So rich in their depths, I find myself staring into them for a moment too long.

"You and the other Earthkin were to be mates of the Atari."

She blinks at me, and I expect her to release a breath of relief. Atari males are renowned for taking great care of their mates. Females are rare and precious beings, after all.

But I should know by now this female does nothing I expect her to do. She is completely like a wild, untamable thing.

Instead of smiling and being relieved at the fact that I am here to bring her to Atar, where she will be loved and cherished by some Atari male desperate to feel her warmth, she throws her head back and howls.

My mouth falls open in surprise as she cackles so hard, she has to grip her belly to steady herself.

"B-bridal gift? Hahaha."

So...this news is what makes water come to her eyes? I watch in further shock as she wipes the tears away.

"Ah, hunky man, you're funny."

"Hunky?" I don't know what this word means.

"Means you're not bad looking. Have a great body too, if what that suit reveals is true."

So...brazen.

I have never witnessed a female compliment a male so openly and I don't know how to respond. And what is this strange feeling across my face? Warmth that makes my skin heat.

"Haaaa..." She stretches out her leg, wincing as she does. "Bridal gift. For a moment, I thought you were serious."

"I *am* serious."

The laughter freezes on her face as she blinks at me.

"Your Earthkin leaders made a deal with us Atari. We were on our way to collect your transport and tow it back to Atar. But the Khuru reached you first."

Her face is unreadable, the smile slowly drying up as she stares at me.

"You are citizens of Atar. You are our responsibility. On behalf of the crown of Atar, I apologize for not finding you sooner."

She blinks then shakes her head. "Citizens of Atar?"

"My home world."

A moment of silence passes between us as she continues staring at me, but I am not sure she is actually seeing me. It appears she is consumed by her thoughts.

"So…it's true then," she finally says. "I wondered why no one from New Earth came after us. I know I'm not the only one who survived. Thought I was just unlucky that I wasn't rescued from those murderers. But…after a while, I told myself it was because, in the grand scheme of things, my life means nothing to those people who live on the Upper Levels. What you're telling me now…is that they…abandoned us."

"Not abandoned—" I begin, but she cuts me off.

"Completely abandoned." And then she laughs. Laughter that is very different from the ones she uttered before. One that is devoid of mirth and soaked in hidden pain.

I know that laugh. Because I have uttered it many times before.

And then she shrugs. She puts the feelings coming to the surface away as if they don't exist. But she is too late, because I have seen them. I know of their presence. And I know they come from a place deep in the soul. One that others don't see. A place that hides from the light.

"Not that I am surprised." She opens another packet of floosh and I watch as it shoots into her mouth. Some of it ends up on her lips and I can't pull my eyes away as her little pink tongue swipes out and collects the jelly.

Hmm.

What is this?

I must have hit my head when I collapsed from the toxin.

"I mean...they abandoned people like me a looong time ago. I just never thought they'd try to ship us off, too."

People like her? "Females?"

"Not females." She gives me a side eye but it has none of the previous defiance and suspicion she often threw my way.

Before I can ask her more, she reaches for the metal pole and uses it to stand.

"Guess I should apologize."

If I wasn't watching her, I might have missed the begrudging way she rolls her eyes.

"You were really only trying to help me."

That huskiness in her voice deepens as she says those words, making a shiver go through my entire frame.

I blink at her.

The toxin is overly affecting my system.

"Want more of this?" She braces on the metal pole and waves a floosh packet at me. I almost drool.

Of all the things in the universe, I could live on floosh for days.

She blows some air through her nose as she crouches on her knee, supporting herself using the pole with ease that only comes with practice as she places the floosh packet against my lips.

I resist the sudden urge to groan when one of her fingers brushes against my fang.

What the qef is happening...?

"Ready?" That husky tone again as she pierces the packet and the floosh shoots into my mouth. I suck it down my throat, almost groaning with pleasure, and she huffs another breath through her nose.

I realize shortly after that it's a subdued laugh when her lips spread and thin as if she's holding back her mirth.

But after seeing that sadness in her eyes only moments before, I want her to laugh.

So when she pulls away, I clear my throat.

"Another."

Her eyes narrow and slide to slits as she looks at me.

"Please."

Why am I begging this female?

She must be a sorceress of some kind.

"Good boy."

Again, that warmth heats my face as I struggle and fight the urge to clear my throat once more.

When she places the packet at my lips, I forget about wanting to make her smile. Instead, all I can focus on is the soft brush of her fingers against my lips as she leans in closer.

"Here you go." The floosh shoots into my mouth and, forgetting what she was doing, I'm caught unaware when the jelly hits the back of my throat. My eyes widen with the sudden feel of the jelly at the back of my throat, and she throws her head back and chuckles.

The sound of her voice...her rich laughter...my face heats like a thousand suns. And what does the female do?

One look at me, and she rises, cackling some more.

Gods help me.

That sensitive skin at the back of my neck pulses, signaling danger and I know it's true.

I am not safe around this female.

Something tells me, she will be the end of me.

7

Mona

So my own planet had planned to sell me off.

Good to know.

Not that I'm in the least bit surprised. Or hurt.

I've been sold off before. My father was the first to do it. Selling his little girl to pay his debts to the scum he owed back on Lower Earth. He'd told her lies too, just like New Earth government had lied about the supposed "cruise".

Luckily, she'd escaped. She'd survived. And just like then, she would survive this without a doubt.

She would get past this because her planet's betrayal wasn't surprising. Trust was earned. Not given. And she shouldn't have expected any better.

As I move around the ship, trying every door I come upon and every storage unit, I try to add as many things as I can to my pile.

I work tirelessly. There's no time to rest because I have no clue when we'll get to the Darzel home world. Every interaction with the ship's AI has returned less than favorable results.

It seems like killing all the Darzel that ran this ship had been a bad idea. But how was I to know they coded the ship to lockdown and return home if none of them were on board? The AI had interacted with me fine before then.

This entire experience is just a big shit show and I can't wait to go home.

My hands pause in the storage locker they're buried inside as I balance on my leg and stretch upward.

There's a sudden lump in my throat that I can't force down.

Home?

If what that Atari stranger said was completely true, then I no longer have a home waiting for me on Lower Earth.

Dropping my hands from the storage locker, I brace against the wall.

That lump in my throat has moved down into my chest, and like an enormous ball filled with lead that presses into my lungs.

I can't breathe.

Swallowing hard, I force myself to focus as I dip my head, a curtain of braids falling to obstruct my view.

I can't breathe.

I need to calm down.

But all I can think of is one thing.

I'm alone again. Hopeless. *Homeless*.

I'm that nine-year-old little girl fending for herself on Lower Earth. No home. No place to go.

Gripping the wall tighter, I force myself to focus because I'm not back where I was twenty years ago. I'm bigger now. Stronger. *Better*.

So why's my body shaking?

I fight to control the tremors. To breathe. But I can't.

The harder I try, the more my chest closes up. The more my lungs burn. Until suddenly, I'm pulled against something hard. Something steady.

Something that seems to suck in all the pain with just one contact.

I inhale deeply, air flooding into my lungs as a hand clasps my neck, forcing my head back as a brawny arm closes around me.

When my vision clears, I see his face.

The stranger. Bhihan of Atar.

He's moving again, the toxin probably worn off, and he's behind me, grasping me to him, those golden eyes of his wild with concern.

For *me*.

I don't even know this male and he's looking at me with more care than I've seen, even in the eyes of my own species.

No one's looked at me like that in so long…

But does he really care, or is this pity?

I stiffen against him, but he does not let me go. Instead, him holding me like this forces me to breathe, and my breaths come hard and heavy.

But I don't want his pity. I'd rather have his anger and his hatred. Anything but his pity.

"Why are you holding me?" I manage the words between breaths as my body is forced to calm down. I can feel his hard body behind me and if it's soaking up all the pain that's being produced in mine and it's such a strange feeling, I don't know how to respond.

He doesn't answer me immediately and I watch as his gaze softens.

"I would purr for you too, but that might anger whichever male is to be your mate."

That knocks all the anxiety out of me in an instant and I release a huge breath before struggling out of his arms. Luckily, he lets me go, otherwise, I'd be stuck in his grasp.

I'd known he was strong, muscular, but feeling every inch of those muscles pressed into my back really paints a good picture of what I'm working with and I am no match for this guy.

"That's not going to happen."

Grabbing my makeshift walking stick, I push away from him, completely aware that he is following behind.

"As soon as you arrive on Atar, many males will flock for your attention. You should prepare yourself for matehood." He pauses. "Some say it's the epitome of existence."

Is that scorn I hear at the edge of his tone?

"I'm not going to Atar."

I swear he grunts.

"And I don't have or want a mate."

He's silent for that one and I almost glance over my shoulder.

My leg hurts as I head toward the bridge and when I reach a step I have to hop down, pain shoots right through it, making me wince.

The stranger is beside me in an instant.

"I've heard you make that sound for possibly a thousand times."

"Okay…" I shift away from him, heading toward my hoard in the center of the room.

"It's annoying."

I grunt, laughter bubbling into my throat. "Sorry to inconvenience you with my pain."

"Pain?" He's beside me again in an instant, and it's either that I'm moving slowly or he is incredibly fast. He bars my path and when I try to move around him, he steps in my way.

I release a breath. "I preferred it when you were paralyzed on the floor."

He ignores me. "Where is the pain?"

I shrug. "It's ok. It's fine." But when I try to move around him once more, my leg betrays me, pain shooting through my thigh that makes me hiss.

The Atari's nostrils flare as he crouches abruptly, large hands grasping my thigh as he investigates. Closing my eyes, I release a breath of defeat.

Even if I could hide it, I shouldn't. Maybe he can help me.

"By the gods!" he almost roars. "This is a kiss from the void."

When he looks up at me, I don't expect to see the utter alarm in his eyes.

He rises abruptly, moving toward the storage panels around the bridge and opening and closing them as he searches for something.

"I've already checked. I couldn't find a first-aid kit."

Once more, he ignores me.

"I can bear the pain."

He looks at me then, golden eyes sliding to me with complete sternness. "I wondered whether you were touched by insanity. You prove me correct at every moment."

I bite my bottom lip.

Maybe in someone else, his words would have made them angry. But for me, the complete bluntness is relieving.

A chuckle bubbles up through my throat. "Me? Insane? Who flew through space on a jet pack toward an incoming ship?"

He frowns at me then. "That was for your sake. Sane females would not have been climbing on the outside of a craft floating in the void."

I shrug. "If I hadn't, you wouldn't have come to rescue me so, win-win." I flash him my most brilliant smile and I swear I see the corners of his lips twist before he growls and turns away from me.

"I would not call that a compensating feature."

I shrug again. "Gotta look at the positives."

Silence descends between us as I watch this huge male move around the bridge, searching through every panel before disappearing into the depths of the ship. He is gone for a few minutes. Long enough that I slide to the floor and rest my head against the control panel.

Jokes aside, this really is a shitty situation. Even as I look at all the shit I piled in the center of the room, I doubt anything will be of use.

When the Atari suddenly walks back into the room, his presence makes me sit up straighter.

He approaches with something in his hand. It looks like gauze at first, until it wobbles on his fingers.

"What's—"

"It should heal your wound."

"Should?"

He crouches before me, reaching for my leg.

"It's goo."

"Didn't you say their goo has toxins?"

"Not this one. This was retrieved from their med bay. It should heal most wounds."

I didn't see a med bay and he must realize that's what I'm thinking because he continues.

"Darzel medicine is not like that of beings that present like Atari. Their med bay is a dome of fluid."

"Ah..." I let the word whisper from my lips as I watch him apply the white goo. I'd seen the dome but had no clue what it was.

As he applies the item, he works slowly and carefully, his gaze completely intent on what he is doing and I find myself staring at this stranger.

This male owes me nothing and if I've learned anything in all my years, it's that generosity comes with a cost.

Always.

So...why is this stranger going out of his way to help me?

8

Bhihan

I'm just finishing tending to the female's leg when I sense a change in the ship.

The atmosphere adjusts. Even with my suit on, I can feel it.

A frown mars my brow as I tilt my head, wondering what exactly I have sensed.

"You feel it too, don't you?" the female suddenly says.

My eyes fly to hers and her brown eyes are pointed at mine.

"The heat. Or the lack of it, rather. It's getting colder in here." Even as she says this, a breath of condensation releases with her words.

Standing abruptly, I look around the room.

She's right. The atmosphere *has* changed and it's because it's getting colder.

Atari aren't susceptible to small temperature changes and as I glance down at the female before me, I wonder just how long the heat has been dissipating.

From her exposed skin, I can tell she feels the cold more easily than I do. Her dark skin is thin. So thin, she might have permanently damaged her leg if she had been out in the void for much longer.

She shivers and I curse under my breath.

Qeffing Darzel.

Their ship is turning off the climate control to conserve energy for the journey because it was not coded to maintain life other than the Darzel that were on board.

I should have imprisoned one of the qeffers inside a storage panel and held him hostage to keep us alive.

"We must move from the bridge."

The female's gaze searches mine. "Why?" Her lower lip quivers and the sensitive flesh at the back of my neck pulses and heats. Alarm runs through me, straightening the hairs along my arms.

The temperature is dropping quickly. Too fast for her body to sustain the change. Even mine. Eventually, I'll begin to shiver like the female before me is shivering now.

"This room is too large. We must conserve heat."

She opens her mouth to say something but closes it shortly after. She knows I am right and when she does not argue like I expect her to, I raise one eyebrow in her direction.

But she does not take the bait of my challenge.

"Where?" she asks.

I don't like the sound her voice has taken. It's lower, but not because it has gone sultry. More like her body is weaker. Tired.

"One of the small storage compartments," I state, moving toward the panel where she'd found the floosh and filling every free pocket on my suit with packets of the delicacy.

Back turned to her, I hear the clang of the metal pole into the ground as she rises and braces on it. When I turn, ready to move with her, the sight of her shivering makes me pause.

Something happens within me. Something that makes me ground my feet so I don't rush toward the female to help her. Make her safe. Ease any discomfort.

This...*urge* is from my cursed Atari lineage. The same one that would make me vow my life to a female that does not want my affection. The same one that makes it almost physically impossible to ignore a female's plight.

I tell myself to stand where I am. To fight the urge. To not let it overcome me. But when the human before me staggers as she tries to make her way toward the corridor, my body defies my mind and I move despite my own command.

When my arms wrap around her, scooping her up, she stiffens even though the growing cold threatens to rack shivers through her frame.

"What are you doing?"

"Hush now, female. Conserve your energy. You will need it."

She shivers some more and concern makes a strange sensation go through me.

Do all humans lose heat this quickly? Only now am I feeling the slight bite of the cold, but for her body to be reacting like this, the temperature must have fallen by several degrees in just minutes.

"Qef," I mutter.

"What does that mean?"

I glance at her. It's not polite to curse around females…but why do I even care? When has it ever mattered before? And why should it matter now?

"Not gonna tell me?" I swear her blunt teeth clatter as she tries to talk, but even in her state, I sense she is trying to be humorous.

She is, once again, not reacting the way I expect her to. Falling apart. Wailing for her mate.

"It is a word that expresses anger and frustration."

"Hmm, like 'fuck'?"

I lift an eyebrow in her direction once more and she chuckles, one that turns into coughs racking her frame. As I make my way down the corridor, kicking in storage panels to find an appropriate spot, she manages to quell the coughs.

"What did you say your name was again?"

I force my attention on finding a place for us to wait out the remainder of this journey and don't bother looking at her jeering little eyes as I answer. "You forget. That means it was not of note to you."

She huffs a breath through her nose that condenses as I walk. "Hey, you don't even know *my* name."

I pause. She has a point. I don't know her name. I had simply been thinking of her as the 'strange rude female'.

"Guess *I* am not of note to you."

She has made a clever point, but when I open my mouth to ask her designation, she makes a sound with her tongue.

"Don't bother asking. Don't expect me to tell you my name now."

"And why is that?" Kicking in a panel, I finally find a space big enough for us both that should help us retain some heat.

"That's just something you will have to earn."

It's my turn to huff a laugh through my nose.

I flew through the void in nothing but the suit on my back to save her. Fought Darzel and was paralyzed by one—a great Atari warrior lying on his face beside Darzel filth. And I am now stuck on a ship heading to my enemies' home world.

And she wants me to do more to earn something as simple as her name?

I want to frown at this female as I duck and crawl into the storage space, still holding her in my arms.

I want to tell her she is ridiculous.

So why is there a stupid grin on my face instead?

9

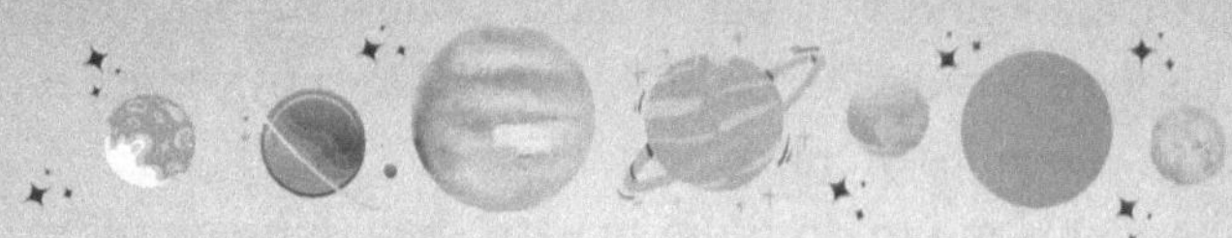

Mona

It's cold. So so cold.

At first, it was just a chill, but in a matter of minutes, it's like I walked naked into a blizzard. My whole body is shivering and I can't stop it. Even the space suit I'm wearing isn't helping. Maybe because that asshole had shot a hole into it.

As the Atari dips and crawls into a small rectangular storage space, I note with a huff through my nose that it looks like a tomb.

Maybe this will be my grave.

Will this be a better death than being torn apart by an oversized warthog?

I contemplate it for a few moments as the alien sets me down on the floor and I'm so cold, I can't even move.

Freezing to death is a bit like falling asleep, right? You don't feel any pain.

I can almost feel my bones rattle as I try to shift and pull my leg up toward my chest, but not even that I can do.

I lie like a block on the floor, shivering, my teeth clattering.

It's jarring, the cold like an icy claw that's covering me from head to toe.

I knew this day would come from the first moment this nightmare began. From the moment the Khuru hijacked our craft and murdered the women around me, I knew death was close.

I'd expected it then. Expected them to slit my throat and end my life. But Dr. Death was biding his time.

So, while they took me against my will across the cosmos, I've held that bean of fear and knowing in my chest. And now, as I lie here on the floor, my limbs slowly turning to ice, I realize that all this time, I have been waiting for it.

I can hardly focus on the alien as he slams the panel to the storage place closed.

He says something and for a moment, I think he is talking to me before I hear the ship's AI respond. Whatever the reply, it makes the Atari pissed because I catch sight of his fangs as he growls. He says something again, fury filling his gaze before his eyes land on me.

"Qef."

Fuck indeed.

He falls to his knees, this male who, now that I have been so close to him, is so incredibly large. He could have snapped me in two already, yet, all this time, I've been jeering and teasing him. Partially to distract myself, and partially because I must have a death wish.

But despite his size, I realize something suddenly. He hasn't used his strength against me once.

A lump forms in my throat as his warm hands grip my waist and flip me on my back.

With his steadiness, his strength, my bones feel like hollow bamboo underneath his palms and tremors I can't control move through me constantly.

His gaze flicks down my frame, his eyes wide as he grips my suit and tugs.

"What—"

My body jerks as he grabs the suit I'm wearing and tugs hard again, stretching the material against my skin almost painfully.

"What are you—"

Why am I unable to finish my sentence? I try again, but my energy is waning. I already can't move and now, even speaking is pulling too many resources. As if my body is doing everything it can to remain warm. Conserving energy. Shutting down all unnecessary functions to keep me alive.

As the Atari dips his head, grasping my suit in his teeth, I would fight back if I could.

I don't know what the hell he's doing, but when he twists his head to the side, his fangs descending at the same time, the movement causes a rip in the fabric, tearing it away from me and revealing my clothes underneath.

He curses again, his brows dipping as he rips my clothes apart.

I try to fight, try to protest, but all that comes from my lips is a weak squeak that makes me feel like a mouse.

What the hell is he doing?

It's cold in here. I am freezing on this ship and he's destroying my clothes, the only thing that is protecting me from the icy air.

As he rips my clothes off me, that lump in my throat freezes with the rest of me as my bare skin is exposed to the cold.

His hands are large. Rough in his ministrations. And for a moment, I leave my body.

My mind takes me back to a place I hadn't been to in a long, long time. A place I'd secured and locked away behind years of walls and barriers.

Running. Running. My bare feet slapping against the pavement, dodging the garbage and shit that litters the streets of Lower Earth. And the sound of heavy footsteps behind me.

The feel of rough hands, one wrapping around my thin prepubescent self. The other slamming over my face, being coated in my tears as they silence my cries.

No one comes to help me.

I have nobody to help me but myself.

No parents. No friends. No home.

I am alone…and he tells me, even as he pulls me into the alleyway, that he will be my friend. That I can live with him. That he will give me a home as long as I be a good girl and give him what he wants.

I try to push the thoughts away. Fuck it, I'm not nine anymore. I've lived through it. Survived it. I'm Mona. Kickass Mona. Mona who can fight and take care of herself.

But despite the strength I draw on, the same strength that has sustained me for years, a sob racks from my throat, a tear escaping from my eye. I feel as the tear freezes on my skin, only making it halfway down my cheek before it turns to ice, and I force my gaze on the Atari before me.

Had I read him wrong?

Was this what he wanted all along?

Had be been waiting until I was helpless, unable to fight back?

Had he…had he been the one to mess with the climate control in the first place, just so this could happen?

All these questions form a whirlwind in my head as I watch the male before me strip his clothes off.

He's perfect. His body something that was carved by the gods themselves. A bronze statue that belongs in the museum of dreams.

Why do this?

A man that looks like him shouldn't want to do this to me. To take from me what I don't want to give.

But as he crouches, reaching for me, I remind myself of the one thing that I have known all my life.

Trust is earned. And no one. No one does anything for free. Generosity *always* comes with a price.

And this Atari has come for payment.

Bhihan

I almost growl in frustration at the look in the female's eyes. Her hatred and fear are undeniable. But I have no time to soothe her or disperse her reservations.

She looks minutes from death and the fact the cold is also biting into my skin only confirms the temperature has gone to dangerous levels.

I strip and fall to the floor, pulling her against me.

Qef.

What's the best way to hold a female when sharing warmth?

I have no mate. I have no clue what to do. Females are so rare on Atar, only the luckiest males have the pleasure of pleasing one.

Despite that, I should *know* what to do.

I might not have a mate, but I am male, and the only thing my body is telling me to do right now is to purr for this female.

Qef me.

For a moment, I resist the urge. But when her ice-cold body touches mine, I know I have to.

Apologizing to the mate I'll never have for this transgression, I pull the female against my skin, wrapping my arms around her and tucking her leg between mine. Tired brown eyes find mine, still filled with hatred and disappointment that make something inside me ache.

"I will not harm you, female."

But my words don't seem to quell her fears. If anything, it makes a fire ignite within those eyes. Such magnificence, the flame that burns in her eyes. Like a torch handed down from the gods, it burns bright and fierce despite that her entire frame is cold and stiff.

And it makes something within me satisfied.

Maybe because I can see she hasn't given up. Maybe because I can see that despite the cold and that her body is shutting down, she still has the will to fight.

Well, fight, little one. Even if it is me that you're taking as your opponent.

So I grip this strange little being. I hold her against me, forcing her to face me as I fold around her. And I purr.

It starts low and deep. A strong vibration in my chest and transfers to the female I am holding, and I pause.

I have never heard my purr before. My growls—those are common. But I have never felt the need to purr for anyone.

For a moment, I relish the sensation. The sound of it, all before the joyous feeling is replaced by reality.

I suppose this is alright.

I will never have a mate. No female to purr to when they are distressed. I might as well use this gift for something. At least one female will benefit from it.

Glancing down, I rest my chin on the strange braids that cover the female's head as I hold her tighter.

That sensitive skin at the back of my neck pulses and heats the more I purr, and I can sense the lessening bite of the cold.

That can only mean one thing. I am heating up, my body generating warmth like a furnace. And as long as I continue to do so, this female will be safe.

I turn with her in my arms and she shivers, her body doing something her mind is fighting against. She snuggles into me despite the war in her eyes.

She does not want my assistance. But as I look down at her, that look in her eyes belies so much more.

This isn't just distrust and annoyance.

For behind her eyes, behind that fire, I can see her pain, her hurt, and deep terror.

I stare at her, puzzled for a few moments as I concentrate on purring to calm her down. And that's when it dawns on me.

My purr stutters at the thought that is now painfully clear.

I stripped this female, her nakedness now pressed against my own, and I forced her body against mine.

In her eyes…what did she think I was doing?

I stiffen, my purr stopping completely as I stare down at her, and as I see the fire dim in her eyes, being replaced by that deep sadness I glimpsed before, my life organ thunders in my chest. An ache goes through me as I growl.

Her gaze snaps to mine, that fire rekindling and I accept it.

But she should know. I am Atari, and no Atari would ever take advantage of a female in the way she must have thought I was about to.

That she was thinking those things makes my anger rise. Not at her, but at myself.

The fact she would think I am that dishonorable is a testament that I have failed my people. My pride almost aches like a physical entity.

I'll do better.

She may be a strange little thing that I have stumbled upon, but I'll take care of her until she arrives on Atar and finds her mate. Until then, I will treat her like the mate I'll never have.

So I hold her, and I start purring again, time slowing down as the cold surrounds her and I maintain us with my heat.

"Whatever thoughts you are having," I whisper, "erase them from your mind. I will never hurt you, female. That isn't the male that I am or will ever be. And I'll prove it to you."

I don't know whether she hears me or not, for I watch as her eyes close, exhaustion winning against the fight her body tries to put up. And when she relaxes against me, her softness going limp as heat returns to her bones, I know I just made her a promise I will keep.

10

Mona

When I wake, it feels like I'm wrapped in a cocoon. Tired eyes open slowly to blurred vision.

I see gray before me and as my vision clears, I realize it's the walls of the small storage space.

My head is cradled by a large hand that presses me against something hard and velvety and as I try to turn, I get a whiff of forest musk.

The alien. The *Atari*. Bean or whatever his name is. He's holding me like a child that's sleeping with its favorite teddy bear—limbs wrapped around me in a death grip—and even as I startle and try to shift, I don't budge.

I'm imprisoned in a cocoon of warmth and the startle and fight that rose within me soon dissipate the moment they arise.

It's so soothing right here. Comfortable.

Despite that his body is like an impenetrable fortress, his velvety skin over the hard muscles almost makes me want to rub against him. And his warmth. It's real, comforting warmth.

How long have we been lying like this?

The question makes me pause, remembering everything that had passed through my mind when he'd first removed my clothes and then his.

I'd thought he was about to drop the good-guy act and show me just how much of a demon he was.

I was wrong. So wrong.

As far as I can tell, he's only been holding me. Keeping me warm. Saving my life. *Again*.

And the way he feels, how naturally he's holding me, as if he's known me for a long time, it all makes something flutter in my chest.

I gulp, pushing back the darkness that had threatened to consume me the moment he'd started taking my clothes off. I'd thought the worst at that moment. The shadows that lurk in the back of my mind coming to the fore.

But now, I'm faced with something else.

The Atari doesn't move and I assume he's asleep. There is only the steady rise and fall of his chest as he breathes. Steady breaths that make *me* rise and fall on his chest as if I weigh nothing.

I'm really like a doll in his arms.

If he'd wanted to do anything to me, he could have. Easily. Instead, he's holding me like someone who actually gives a fuck.

I swallow hard once more, forcing myself to keep still and not freak out.

But apart from all my previous reservations about this male, there is something else that threatens to make me withdraw and pull into myself.

As he breathes, the movement is a glaring indicator he is, indeed, real. And the sensation of someone this close…someone *holding* me…it makes me want to stiffen. Every hair on my body standing on end as I wait for something *bad* to happen.

When was the last time that I was held like this?

I try to remember. I try to recall days when someone cradled me in their arms and made me feel safe. Days when I didn't have to rely only on myself.

But I can't remember.

Even going as far back as my childhood, no memories like this surface.

It is an unnatural sensation, being held. One that makes me want to fight to get out of his grasp and another that makes this skin-to-skin contact utterly terrifying.

The fear almost consumes me. Simply because this feeling, this sensation, it's…comforting.

Just like how he'd held me before when panic almost consumed me.

Tears well in my eyes and I refuse to let them fall.

Had I always been this on edge? This easily frayed?

Had all these emotions always been this close to the surface?

Or, is there something about this male that is bringing out the worst in me?

I sniffle, a shiver going through me and the male holding me moves in his sleep.

A rumble goes through his chest as he pulls me impossibly closer and even as I stiffen, unwilling to let my guard down, he simply holds me close.

One of his hands slips down to where he'd treated my leg with that strange goo and he mumbles something in his sleep.

"—will stop hurting soon, little one. Bhihan is here."

I freeze, eyes widening…but he's not awake.

I sniffle again, another shiver going through me and he rolls, adjusting himself on the floor. A rumble goes through his chest, almost like a deep purr as he threads his fingers through my braids with the hand that's cradling my head.

"Hush now, little one. I am here. I'll keep you safe."

I know he isn't aware of what he's saying, so why are tears slowly gathering in my eyes?

"Bhihan is here," he mumbles again before his purr dies down to be replaced by his steady breaths.

I gulp, pushing down the ball of emotions rising in my throat as I force my shoulders to relax.

He isn't harming me. He isn't doing anything except comforting me.

Throughout all this nightmare, ever since the moment I left New

Earth on that cruise, I had thought this was all a precursor to my doom.

But this comfort. This warmth. I know this is only for a few moments and that as soon as he wakes, it will end. And I feel guilty as I snuggle into his warmth and take the comfort he is giving me.

A single tear escapes down my cheek as I let my head relax. I can almost feel a crack in the center of my chest, in the walls I've built to protect myself, as I allow myself to accept this stranger's kindness.

11

Bhihan

Something wakes me, and for a moment my mind is muddled. Did I fall asleep?

It's startling, enough for me to jerk awake fully.

This is unheard of. When was the last time I fell asleep so easily? Even tucked into my quarters on the Zarzenius, I lay awake during rest cycles staring at the void through my window panel.

To fall asleep now so easily…

It must be because of the cold.

I shift and a little whimper makes my ears perk.

Something soft struggles against me and I freeze again.

"A little room, big guy? You're going to squish me."

The female.

Looking down, deep brown eyes meet mine as she offers me a slight smile. The sight of her there, the feel of her body pressed into mine, is enough to make me jerk, thrusting her away from me.

Her eyebrows shoot up in surprise as she wraps her arms around her chest immediately, a shiver going through her frame.

"*You* were the one holding *me*, you know. I didn't crawl into your arms."

She's right.

I remember tearing her clothes off, desperate to get to her skin so I could share my warmth.

I'd stripped bare, pulling her against me so I could save her life. And I...I *purred*.

My hand moves to the center of my chest as I stare at her, the memory feeling like a strange one. As if it was someone else that did all those things and not me.

Almost as if some craze had taken my consciousness and rendered me a slave only to my instincts.

When my gaze dips, falling down her frame, she curls in on herself a little, more shivers moving through her.

Qef.

I'm an idiot.

Reaching for her, she startles just before I wrap my arms around her and pull her into me once more. Small shivers still go through her frame as I settle her in my arms, and for a moment, neither of us speaks.

"It's only to keep you warm—"

"Thanks for keeping me warm—"

We speak at the same time and fall into silence once more.

"I..." Now with her back turned to me, she pulls her arms around herself and dips her chin toward her chest. "I would have frozen to death if you didn't help me."

I don't say a thing. I do not know what to say. I can't berate her and I can't accept her gratitude.

I did what any sane Atari would do.

"You don't have to thank me for this."

She shakes her head, the strange braids in her hair brushing against my chest.

"I do. You've saved me several times in such a short time."

I grunt.

For a moment, I look down at her, enjoying the fact she isn't glaring up at me with the hurt and pain I'd seen in her eyes before she'd fallen asleep. Now, it seems those terrible emotions are gone. Replaced by some sort of resignation that even influences the way she speaks.

Her words leave her lips like soft wisps. As if she's been thinking about things for a while, reflecting on this whole ordeal.

"You must think I'm reckless."

I tilt my head slightly.

Do I?

"I think you are fearless."

Her head snaps back quickly, so she can look up at me. Surprise shines in her widened eyes. "Fearless?"

"I have never seen a female brave the void of space to circumvent hostiles. You could have remained in the vessel. Waited to see if someone would rescue you."

She snorts. "I refuse to wait for some man to rescue me."

It's a strange sound that only highlights how much smaller than me she is. I never noticed it before. I wasn't looking at her in that light.

But she is a small female. Long limbs, but they are thin.

She brings her leg up, tucking it toward her chest and I adjust my arms so I wrap around her more, waiting for the moment she realizes she is still unclothed.

We know of the Earthkin's modesty laws. Atari have no such rules.

Here, I am as much in my element without my garments as I am when I am clothed. But she...her nakedness is something that will cause her alarm as soon as she notices.

I suppose the fact she hasn't yet caused a ruckus is because she is still in shock.

"It was your fault, wasn't it?"

"Hm?" She glances up at me once more, her eyes like something dark and sweet that beckon to me and I frown as soon as our gazes linger for too long.

She frowns back before looking away, and tension swells between us.

"What's my fault?"

"This vessel leaving hyper speed so suddenly." I clear my throat "Not even the Darzel are that reckless."

She shrugs. "Maybe. I didn't want to go to their world. I know what happens as soon as I get there."

So she knows what the Darzel do…and she is so calm about it?

A breath causes her shoulders to rise and fall and I note she isn't shivering anymore. But the movement makes her body writhe against mine and that fleshy bit at my nape pulses. Probably with irritation.

"But I never imagined I'd be lying naked in the arms of a stranger either." She shrugs again. "I just have to take it as it goes. I realized a long time ago that…"

I wait for her to continue but instead, her lips press into a thin line before she huffs a soft laugh through her nose.

"Nevermind."

I tilt my head, studying her. "Continue. I wish to listen."

"You don't need to hear what I was going to say. It's a bit discouraging at best."

I study her some more.

That tone in her voice. The resignation.

"What did you realize a long time ago?"

This time, when I speak she slowly turns so she's looking at me. Her eyes rove over my brow, my nose, my lips, taking in my features in such a way that makes me aware of my own face.

"I realized that fighting against destiny is futile. I take the moments as they come. The days as they're presented to me. When I was young, I used to try and change things, fighting against what's already set… now I know better."

Her words make me think.

"You believe destiny is set."

She nods. "Don't you?"

I nod slowly and her eyebrows move up a notch.

"I see." She whispers. "I wonder what made you come to that realization."

Her eyes dip as she stares at the floor and we slide into another pocket of silence. It's comfortable silence. The type that's hard to gain with strangers. Even with my brothers, Qhenno, Aqnar and the prince, Da'red, it can be difficult to not try and fill the silence with words.

But with this strange female. I have no urge to.

I can feel the shadows that bind her as strongly as I feel my own, even as her words swirl in my head. And I want to answer her.

I wonder what made you come to that realization.

"You wonder why I think destiny is set," I whisper, and she turns her head slightly so I know she's listening.

There is no hatred in her eyes now. No fight. She is as bare as her nakedness before me. And maybe that's why my lips move. Why I keep talking even when I'd have stilled my tongue in another situation.

"Because, for me, little female…it has always been written in stone. For me, destiny can never be changed."

12

Mona

I don't know whether this dude is a big marshmallow or someone I should be wary of anymore.

When I came in and saw him killing those Darzel, I could see in the way he moved he is a force to be reckoned with if he chooses. Even sitting with him now, his large frame takes up almost all the space in this little room, and yet, he holds me so gently.

Apart from the moment he woke up and thrust me off him like I was trash.

But he pulled me back as soon as he realized what he'd done.

I have never been more confused by a male's actions as I am by this one's.

Which male in their right mind puts themself in so much danger for a stranger?

The answer comes to me almost immediately.

A male who has nothing to lose.

I look at him as he speaks, his words taking on more meaning than I think he realizes.

Something about him makes another layer of my guard fall.

If I'm not certain of anything else, one thing is clear. He has a good heart.

I'd be dead several times over if that wasn't the case.

As he shifts and takes out one of the jelly packets from his pocket, he nicks it easily with his fang, and I'm surprised the jelly doesn't shoot out like it does when I do it. I realize shortly after that's because it's almost frozen solid.

The alien grips it with the side of his mouth and breaks off a piece before swallowing the chunk, his gaze falling to me...and then to my lips.

He stares at them for far too long, far past what is polite, and it causes me to lick my lips out of pure self-consciousness.

He shifts again, forcing me back against him as his hand comes around, presenting what's left within the packet at my lips.

It's my turn to shift as I try to free my hands from his grasp, but he's wrapped himself around me again. It keeps me warm. Very warm. But I can hardly move.

And how comes he's not affected by the cold like I am?

I'm about to ask him to ease up when the hardened jelly is pressed against my lips.

"Wha...I can feed myself if you just release me." I struggle again, but there is no give. Instead, the food is pressed against my lips again. Silence on his end.

Shrugging slightly, I release a soft breath.

I guess it doesn't matter.

But when I open my mouth and his hand moves forward, it's like the air around us changes.

He does it so slowly, sliding the piece of jelly from the packet into my mouth, that I have my mouth open, my tongue stuck slightly out for long enough that the whole thing causes warmth to spread across my cheeks.

As soon as the food touches my tongue, he pauses and I have to tilt my head forward to take the rest of it into my mouth.

He's looking at me strangely now, those golden eyes set underneath a furrowed brow. But it isn't annoyance in his gaze like before. It's confusion.

Maybe he's seen my teeth and realizes I don't have fangs?

But it's not that. He shivers. For the first time, he shivers like the cold is finally settling into his bones and I swear I feel a chill go across his skin.

And then I feel something else.

Something large and hard, impossibly hard, suddenly rises between us, pressing into my back with a force that startles even me.

"What is—"

But as I try to jerk away from him to investigate what's happening, he holds me tighter, the packet of jelly falling from his fingers as his eyes widen and he freezes with me in his arms.

"Are you alrigh—"

Oh fuck.

As that hard thing heats against my spine, I finally realize what it is. I hadn't felt it before. Granted, I wasn't thinking about nakedness and body parts when my sole focus was on keeping my organs from freezing over. But how could I ignore it now?

His cock presses into my spine. Prods. Pushes. As if seeking something, and it's my turn to stop moving.

The ship shudders and I can't even pull my attention away from the alien behind me.

A pained sort of look goes across his face as his eyes fill with growing fear that holds me silent. He isn't doing it on purpose, that is clear. It seems, he's even as embarrassed as I am shocked about it. And there's a growing look of horror on his face as he rubs a large palm across his nape, his eyes widening further as a groan, or is it a moan, rumbles in his chest.

"Bhihan?"

His eyes focus on me with intense clarity at the sound of his name. I guess I memorized it after all. After he kept repeating how he'd keep me safe and whatnot in his sleep.

The ship shudders again, enough for my gaze to flick from his to the walls around us.

The distinct hum of the engines stutters and winds down, almost like the sound of a huge turbine slowing down.

"We're exiting hyper speed..." I murmur and all that anxiety I'd pushed away and tried to forget about comes rushing back. As does the heat.

The bite of the cold outside of Bhihan's arms begins to lessen as the engines slow down.

We're arriving?

Already?

But the alien holding me close doesn't react to any of this. When I look at him again, he's staring at me as if he's seeing a ghost. His cock throbs in my back like an insistent entity and it hits me that I haven't struggled to get away from it, or him.

Why doesn't this obviously sexual part of him make me want to flee?

Maybe because throughout all this, the only thing he's forced me to do is eat some jelly?

Again, is he a big guy with a soft heart or someone I should be afraid of?

When his cock pulses and he lets out a strangled, pained sort of groan, my heart skips a beat.

"Are you alright?"

I'm going to ignore the rod between us for now. There are more pressing things at hand. But instead of answering me, Bhihan releases me suddenly.

He almost staggers away from me, crawling on the back of his arms as he puts distance between us.

The Atari is now staring at me as if I am a dangerous creature and my brow furrows. Why's he acting like this so suddenly?

Yes, he got hard. That's natural, isn't it?

My gaze falls to land between his legs and I can feel my face go blank.

What in the fuck?

His cock is nothing like I expected it to be.

It's larger. Thicker. Harder than what should be possible.

Ridges run up the shaft to culminate at the flared head and even as I stare at it, it bobs to slap into his lower belly in an obscene display of both strength and raw sexuality.

When my eyes fly to his, I expect to see a cocky disposition. Maybe a wink. Definitely a challenge.

I get none of that.

What I see is pure raw fear. So evident it's almost tangible.

Not even when we'd realized we were stuck on this ship, heading possibly to our deaths did this alien look scared.

But now. He is absolutely terrified.

The trouble is, I have no clue what's causing this sudden change in his behavior.

The ship shudders again, harder this time, and I have to pull my gaze away from his.

"We're arriving, I think."

My heart thumps hard in my chest, uncertainty about what comes next taking the forefront of my mind.

I know we're arriving. We have to be, because the climate control has kicked in again and it's no longer biting cold.

Reaching for what's left of my clothes, I have to steady my hands and stop myself from trembling as I rifle through them.

But they're all ripped. Unwearable.

A tunic lands on my leg and I turn to see he's pulling on the suit he was wearing. He's no longer meeting my eyes, focusing solely on getting himself dressed. A growl goes through him that makes the hairs along my arms rise.

It's anger. Pure raw anger. As sudden and surprising as the look of terror that had held him frozen just moments before.

As he tries to hurry, his cock bobs, giving him a hard time getting it within his suit. He doesn't touch it, instead using the back of his wrists to push it inside while he secures the suit. Almost as if he is afraid to touch himself.

It's all so curious, I find myself staring in his direction for far too long, until the ship shudders so hard, it almost displaces my position.

"Entering Darzel air space." The voice of the AI is loud, and I grab Bhihan's tunic and pull it over my head, thrusting my arms inside it.

It hangs on me like a robe and the scent of sweet forest rain is embedded in the fibers, but I don't even care.

We're arriving.

And that can only mean one thing.

I'm about to be enslaved again and possibly be fed to a wild animal.

But that was my fate before we killed the Darzel on board.

What will they do to us now that we've killed their own?

13

Mona

A shudder goes through the ship like the craft is being pulled by something other than itself, and I stagger, kneeling as I reach out to the wall for balance.

Shit.

Shit shit shit shit shit.

"We're screwed." I look at the alien and a lump forms in my throat when I turn to find him staring at me.

No. At his tunic.

The arms are so large, mine swim in them.

His gaze lifts almost slowly, and I wish I could understand the look in his eyes. It's a mixture of fear, distress, anger, and…longing. That last one though, it's almost so faint, I would have missed it if I didn't spend most of my life reading people's expressions to survive.

Back on Lower Earth, it's hard to find people to trust. Everybody is out for their own gain. Reading what's behind the eyes becomes a valuable skill.

One I learned to rely on.

And now, it's telling me this alien has something he's hiding. Something he's battling with that's suddenly come to the fore.

Well, we'll have to deal with that later because we're about to become warthog meat.

"Do you think they'll check in here? Like, could we hide in here and maybe they'll miss us?"

He doesn't answer immediately, but his throat moves. He's still giving me that strange look, and the intensity in his eyes hasn't changed.

"Bhihan?"

Fear again, in his eyes, at the sound of his name on my lips.

The ship jerks and grinds to a halt and I have to push whatever he's going through to the back of my mind.

"We have to do something."

I look around the room, but it really is simply like a box. Only two small holes in the roof, just big enough for my palm to cover them, interrupt the smoothness of the walls.

I brush my hand over one and feel the pull of air.

They are air vents. And there's nothing else apart from those in this small space.

Maybe if I block them up, when the Darzel enter they won't smell us.

Bracing my back against the wall, I slide to the floor so I can take the pressure off my knee, my chest heaving as I try to think of a plan.

I can't cover the vents. That's a stupid idea. We'd probably suffocate if I do that.

And that means we also can't stay in this room. What happens when the ship's no longer running and the vents stop pushing air inside? We'd suffocate then too.

Fuck.

"Guess we have to go out there…"

"Yes." The deep voice that answers me makes my gaze fly back to the Atari.

He's crouching stiffly, still with as much distance as he can place between us, and now he's deliberately not meeting my gaze.

Is he really that embarrassed about getting a hard-on?

If anything, *I'm* the one who should be offended.

Or, maybe that's just it. Maybe he *is* offended and not because of his hard-on, but because of me.

Being around him for such a short time, I can already tell that whatever world he's come from is different from my own.

Is he upset that his body responded to a female like me? One that's classed as *lower* by my own people?

I study him, my eyes narrowing when he looks at me but pulls his gaze away again.

If that's the case…then fuck him.

"Fine," I say, easing my back off the wall.

The ship rumbles again as the engine slowly dies and I swallow hard, pulling on the strength I've always had to muster. The same strength that's kept me going all these years.

I can do this.

"They will board soon." His gaze is focused on the door panel and a sense of *something* goes through me. Loss? Sadness?

Was I starting to like this alien?

As he reaches forward and pushes against the panel so it opens enough to let him through, I watch as he exits, counting the seconds that pass. When he lifts the panel again and glances in at me, I jerk my head in a nod, more to myself than to him, and climb out after him.

A strong hand grasps my hand and helps me into a standing position as soon as I exit the storage panel, but I try not to look at him. I don't want to see that look I've become so accustomed to seeing in others' eyes. The one they have when it's time to move on and they've thrown me away.

Because I am sure it will be there in his.

This is where we part ways.

I am a slave and he is…

I don't know what he is, but he certainly isn't in the same boat as me.

There's a sound in the back of the ship that makes me startle but I only get to turn my head in that direction before I'm hopping beside the alien as he leads me the other way.

A curse sounds under his breath as he dips and scoops me into his arms, moving down the corridor far faster than I could ever have.

The sounds coming from the back of the ship increase and by the time the Atari falls into a seat on the bridge, settling me to face him on his lap, my heart's hammering in my chest in expectation for what comes next.

They're going to come on the ship.

They're going to notice their people are dead.

And they're going to find us sitting on the bridge like we own the place.

With wide eyes, I stare at the Atari but his gaze is focused down the corridor.

I hear the sounds of the Darzel coming on board just seconds later and a nervous shiver goes through me.

One of the Atari's hands comes up my back, skimming my spine as a deep rumble develops in his chest. And it shouldn't, but just the sound of it is calming the erratic beats of my heart.

I find myself studying him, fighting to keep my breaths steady despite the sounds of the Darzel approaching. And just when they come into earshot, the golden pits of the Atari fall on me.

Bhihan gazes into my eyes with a look I'm almost afraid to decipher before the hand at my back presses hard, forcing my chest against his as his head dips and his lips capture mine.

Shock goes through me, enough to hold me frozen, my eyes wide at the sensation of his hot lips against mine.

His tongue swipes into my mouth almost hesitantly as he stares back at me and for a moment, the world stands still.

I don't know what he's doing, but as his tongue flicks again, brushing against mine, a rumble goes through his frame that threatens to make me close my eyes and whimper into his mouth.

I don't know what the fuck's happening, but I can't fight it. Because he makes sure I can't.

The hand at my back forces me to tilt my head back and accept his lips, while his other hand snakes around my thigh to clasp the round curve of my ass, pressing my crotch down against his.

This is wrong. He can't just take what he wants from me. He's not allowed to…*use* me.

And it's certainly not the time!

Once more, a part of me wonders if this is what he wanted all along. If I'd once again mistaken the meaning behind his generosity. And that makes me struggle against him. But the Atari only kisses me harder.

His lips swirl against mine as another rumble goes through his chest, the sound of it sending a distinct throb through me.

I don't know why, and maybe it's madness, maybe it's the fear of my impending death, maybe it's both, but I flick my tongue against his.

It's only once. Only tentative, but I see fire flash in his eyes as he stares back at me.

They say it's impolite to kiss someone with your eyes open.

So why is the fact he's kissing me now while his gaze locks with mine keeping me hypnotized?

Possibly because this isn't just any kiss.

This isn't even a kiss at all.

I don't know his end game, but the moment my tongue flicks against his is the moment I hear the Darzel enter the bridge behind us.

Everything the Atari is doing to me fades into the background as I hear our enemy behind us. But for the Atari before me, they might as well not exist.

With a rumble, his kiss intensifies as he pulls me closer, gripping my ass and squeezing it as if it belongs to him.

"Halt!" One of the Darzel says and I stiffen.

But the Atari ignores them. Or maybe he doesn't hear that they're right here, in the same room as us.

His lips are incredibly soft as his tongue brushes against mine, another rumble going through him that pulls me back into his world.

For he's kissing me like he never wants to stop.

I don't get it. I don't understand what the hell is happening in his head. First he looks at me like I'm offensive to him and then—

A moan escapes from my lips when his hand slips up to the nape of my neck, grasping it as he tilts my head back and thrust his tongue down my throat.

"You there!"

I can hear the Darzel have come closer, but now, they are in the background of my mind. No longer in the present. Hardly consequential as Bhihan kisses me, the invasion of his tongue forcing me to focus on him, the smoldering heat in his gaze putting me in a trance.

No one has ever looked at me the way Bhihan is looking at me right now.

"What is an Atari doing on our ship?!"

"Hostile!" Another says. "Several Darzel are dead. Found in a storage bay."

I can sense the Darzel are staring at us and only then does Bhihan pull his lips from mine.

He leaves me panting, my gaze searching his for answers. But those smoldering eyes suddenly go hard.

They cut off as if I'd imagined it all, turning to ice as he shifts his gaze behind me.

"Notify the king," I hear one of them whisper. "Make haste."

There is shuffling as one of them hurries away and Bhihan's gaze shifts. But he's still not looking at me. It's as if I no longer exist.

What the hell is happening here?

"How dare you, Atari..." the Darzel begins, but his words fade off as soon as Bhihan sits up straight, bringing me with him, but I'm not even sure he knows I am still here.

His focus is completely on the aliens in front of him.

"H-how dare you," the Darzel continues. "You have slaughtered our people and here you sit performing obscene mating rituals among their corpses!"

Bhihan shrugs, his large shoulders rising and falling as his gaze flicks from one Darzel to the other.

I'm not surprised when the Darzel releases a sound of anger. "Seize him! According to Darzel law, he must be sentenced to death."

Oh shit.

I reckon there are at least two of them and when I glance over my shoulder, I see I am correct.

My gaze flicks around to find the metal pole I've been using as a tool. Maybe we can kill them and find some way off this planet that does not include this ship.

"Seize him!" the Darzel commands again, but his kin at his side only moves partway, gaze flicking from Bhihan to the one in charge and back.

"I have a better proposition," Bhihan says.

My gaze flashes back to his. Are we really in the position to be proposing anything right now?

"This is my mate."

I blink at him. What now?

"She is mine and that means she is Atari. But you stupidly captured her. Brought her harm."

Huh?

His fingers tighten on my ass as if to say I shouldn't open my mouth so I force it closed, but I'm glad I'm facing him because the look in my eyes would give us away.

"Mate?" The surprise in the Darzel's voice echoes the same surprise going through me.

"I can assure you we did not remove her leg," the other Darzel says. "Preliminary reports sent from this ship indicate the prisoner was already injured. But it did not mention you were on board. We believe—"

"Do I look like I care what you believe?" Bhihan's fingers tighten some more on my butt, enough that I fear he'll leave an imprint there. There's a fire blazing in his eyes and even though his voice is calm, a tension radiates from him that tells me if he snaps, all of those Darzel are going to die.

"She is Atari," he repeats, "and you took her." There is silence from the Darzel and as Bhihan continues, I hold my breath, anticipating his every word. "On Atari law, I had reason for slaughtering your kind."

When I glance back their way, I can see the Darzel visibly shifting away.

"B-but you are on Darzel home world now. Your law does not work here."

Bhihan shrugs. "You seem to misunderstand. I really don't care what you believe."

That makes the Darzel's eyes widen slightly. "Our King will not have this!"

Bhihan shrugs again, his gaze growing bored.

"Fine," he says. "Bring me to him."

As he rises, still holding me so I'm straddling his waist, the Darzel take a few steps back, heads tilting so they can look up at the Atari warrior now looming over them.

"F-follow us."

14

Bhihan

The female in my arms is my mate.

And I? I am a useless male who is a fool.

I knew it the moment my fangs suddenly filled with life spirit. Almost bursting from the tips as realization overcame me.

As I grip her to me, her soft body molds around mine as if she was made to be there. And that's because she is. Qef me. She is.

This rude, annoying little thing…is *mine*. And I know that, even with her hatred for me, I would not change her for the world.

It is clear now. Was I only able to stay in her presence because I secretly enjoyed it?

For a moment, I steel myself against the barrage of feelings suddenly battering me. I was an idiot to not realize this as soon as I touched her skin. I should have understood the tightening at the back of my neck was not because we were in danger. That the heat going through my flesh was not because of the cold.

How could I not notice until my cock forced me to? Until it became so stiff I could not ignore it?

Because I've been convinced for so long that this would never happen. That I was undeserving of a mate bond. Because *I am*. And for that reason, I have done everything so that it does not happen.

But this…this unexpected occurrence has caused the one thing in the universe that I am afraid of. And now I am consumed by a single thought.

I must protect her from my curse.

I must protect her from *me*.

As I carry the female, following the Darzel outside the ship, I keep my gaze forward.

I can't meet her deep, questioning eyes. I can't look at her because I am afraid she will see it all.

The pain. The shame. The fear that's held me captive since I became of age and realized the fates have cursed my kin.

That my bloodline only brings pain and that I must be the one to end the pain carried through the generations.

I must have no mate. And yet, one clings to me right now.

Mine.

A female for my own.

My fangs hurt even just holding her like this, begging me to mark her.

I grip her tighter and she doesn't complain, but I can feel her gaze.

I have confused her. Pressing her lips against mine, *tasting* her, had been a bad idea. I'd done it to distract the Darzel, but now, I want more.

How can a male go so long not knowing he wants something as badly as one taste of this female has awakened within me?

For a moment, while my tongue brushed against hers, I forgot about the danger. I forgot about the pain only I could feel.

And she felt good. Too good.

I am undeserving…and it was wrong for me to take. To taste her.

For she is my mate…and that means the fates have cursed her, too. The mate of Bhihan of Atar will only be brought pain, and I have already seen the pain behind her eyes.

She has already experienced too much hardship. Too much strain.

Why have the fates given her to me to be cursed with more?

I swallow hard, keeping my gaze forward as we exit the vessel.

Bright light from the star hits me in the face, enough to make me squint.

The Darzel home world is one where the star shines with such vengeance, their earth is dry and dusty. Lucky for them, the goo they excrete protects their skin from the treacherous rays.

But we have no such protection. Neither me nor my female...

I growl at the reference.

My female?

The fates may say she is mine, but I can't accept her. I have to make her reject the bond. *Somehow*. I must cause her to hate me even more than she already does. It will be better for us both.

But even as I follow the Darzel down a path leading away from the ship and more of their kind stop in their tracks at our arrival, I see none of that. All I can feel is the tense female in my arms and the urge to comfort her is almost overpowering.

Foolish Bhihan. You have lived for so many orbits and you are no smarter than a kit.

You *purred* for her.

That should have been the first indicator.

Never have I felt the urge to do such a thing, but even then, I was so convinced it would never happen, I didn't see it coming until it was right upon me.

My time on the Zarzenius, spending all my days in the void and away from my people, *females*, so I don't trigger any bonds...all of that has been for naught when the first female I have encountered in so many moons happens to be the one fated for me.

Qef. Me.

I hold her closer still, not allowing her to pull away even though she has no idea what the qef has happened between us. If this is the only time I'll have her in my arms, I will treasure it for as long as it lasts. For soon, she will want nothing to do with me. Which I accept.

The last thing I want to do is hurt her. Bring her pain.

But I berate myself once more. It took yoras of having her bare skin against mine before those instincts I was pushing back came to the fore. If I had not stripped us both, maybe I would not have realized this...

Maybe ignorance of this bond would have been for the better.

Only, I could not have let her freeze to death.

"Bhihan…"

Her whisper makes a part of me ache. The way she says my name is not normal. No one says my name like that. And when did she start calling me by my name anyway? That husky voice makes it sound sensual instead of simply a sound to gain my attention.

"Bhihan." More forceful this time and I have no choice but to dip my gaze to hers.

Big mistake.

Wide brown eyes are looking at me as if I have gone insane. But what I don't see there is fear.

Because of course. The female the fates chose for me is fearless. Strong. A fighter.

Perfect for *me*.

Another ache goes through me, but I push it away.

Make her hate me. That's what I have to do.

I should let her walk, but she doesn't have her pole. If I set her down now, will that incite vitriol within her?

Possibly.

I stop walking, contemplating it, but even as logic says I should set her down…I cannot.

The thought of her limping, struggling to keep up with us is too much for me to bear.

Qef. I really am a useless male.

So I hold her still, my brows diving at my weakness.

"What is it?" I growl, and she cocks an eyebrow at me.

"What the fuck is your game plan here?"

I hardly hear her words. Now, outside of the artificial lights of the Darzel vessel, she is even more striking than before. The star's rays kiss her and her dark skin glows.

She is stunning.

"Bhihan!"

The skin on my jaw pinches, and I stare at her in shock.

"Hey! I'll resort to more than pinching you," she whispers harshly, "if you don't answer me. Pay attention! We're walking into a very dangerous situation here."

I stretch my jaw. For such small hands, that hurt.

She glares at me, her eyes widening even more as she brings her face close. "You don't have a plan, do you?"

A laugh huffs from my nose before I can stop it. I'm supposed to be strict with her. Angry. Ruthless. Someone she hates. And I am failing before I have even started.

The path curves and opens up on a busy street. Tall dirt structures rise from the ground and I feel when my female stiffens even more in my arms.

It must look very alien to her.

As far as I know, her planet has not traveled to many other worlds. All communication they receive has been through visits from other beings to their planet.

But even to me, one who has visited many planets, the Darzel home world is a wonder to behold.

The same dirt that flies in the wind is the one they have used to build every structure as far as the eye can see. It's an expanse of brown that isn't interrupted by anything except the sea of green Darzel mulling about. Most of whom stop as soon as they see us.

Interested eyes turn our way and I can already see their hunger for blood. They might not do well in one-and-one combat—their only real defense being their toxic goo—but what they can't do themselves, they love to see in the middle of their arena.

Poor creatures ripped apart for their entertainment.

And I am sure that is where we will end up.

I might be Atari, but I have no way of getting out of this situation with no ship and no weapons. I might as well be defenseless.

The only way I can think of us getting to the end of this alive is to play the Darzel's games. And until then, I'll just have to pretend.

"Bhihan?"

A sense of trepidation shoots through me. And the worst thing, it's not for myself, but the female clinging to me.

Qef me. How will we survive this when my thoughts will be consumed by her?

As I open my mouth to answer her, the Darzel leading us stops before a set of great doors. His beady eyes slip to me before focusing on my female, the jewels he's wearing jingling as he turns, and I can see the calculations going through his eyes even without him speaking.

If he thinks he will separate us, he should also imagine losing a few limbs because I'll rip him apart if he tries to take her from my arms.

"Hush, female." I make my voice as gruff as I can, hoping she realizes I'm pretending, but at the same time, wanting her anger all the same. I *need* her anger. Because if she gives me any favor, I might not make it. "You are mine to do with as I please, and I speak so these Darzel hear. Slow your tongue and speak only at my request." I pull my gaze to hers, expecting to see the vitriol beginning. Again, I am wrong.

Instead, she cocks another eyebrow at me, her lips curling at the corners as she gives me a challenging look. I stiffen.

If she blows the cover I'm trying to create…

But as suddenly as the look came over her features, it disappears. Her face softens and her lips spread into a soft smile.

She lifts a hand to my jaw and makes a sound in her throat that makes my cock harden in my suit.

"Oh my lord, forgive me." She pushes up her lips and my arms tremble. "I am but your humble servant."

I have to fight to prevent my mouth from falling open.

If I didn't know her, know the exact menace that she can be, I would believe her sudden change in demeanor.

And the bad thing, her sweet words are doing nothing for my control.

Qef me.

My situation…is hopeless.

15

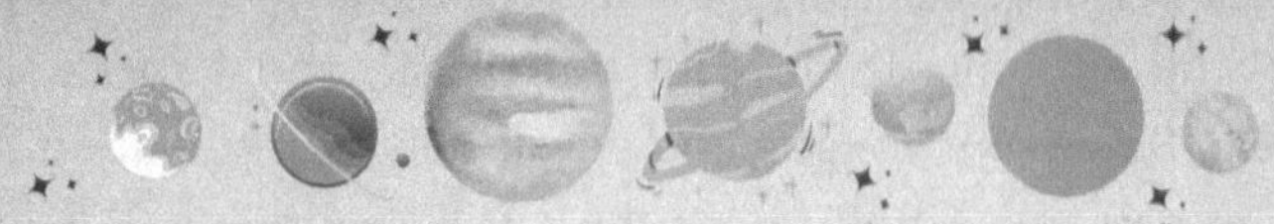

Mona

Whatever game he's playing. I can play along. And I'll put on my best act. After all, our lives depend on it.

Bhihan obviously knows more about these Darzel than I do, so I'll go along with whatever he's trying to do.

It's clear to me now what that kiss was about. He wants them to think we are mates, and I don't know why, but I can roll with it.

I can adjust.

It's what I do.

What I can't come to terms with, however, was the way my body reacted to him. And it isn't helping when he's still carrying me straddling him.

His palms flex against the curve of my butt, and I give myself a mental shake.

Just an act.

We can do this.

As huge doors open to let us through, I keep my face tucked against this male who flew into my life at the exact moment that I needed him, and I put my trust in him. Putting my life in his hands without questioning it.

But none of that is hard to do. Because it's easy to trust Bhihan.

It's a revelation that has me floored as he walks through the doors into what looks like a large, sparse courtyard.

Jewels hanging on stalks glint in the bright sunlight at what, I guess, is their version of a garden. Because what grows on this desert planet?

All I have seen so far are mounds of dirt, mountains of dirt, pillars of dirt, and more dirt.

What do these beings even eat?

How do they survive?

There are so many of them, there has to be a water and food source *somewhere*.

Bhihan stops walking, and the stream of Darzel following behind us stops, too. I have a view behind his back and they're all staring at him with a hungry look in their eyes. And then that hungry look shifts to me almost collectively.

It sends a shiver down my spine.

Again, I don't know how we're going to get out of this.

Fighting a few Darzel might have been possible, but a whole city?

Nope.

"Oh great king, we bring to you the fiend that killed your heir!"

My eyes bug out and I turn to see the huge Darzel I'd seen on the holo vid sitting right there on a raised dais.

His heir?!

I stare at Bhihan, but he has a bored sort of annoyed look on his face.

We killed the king's son?! Could this get any worse?

I wouldn't be surprised if he sentenced us to death right here, right now. No questions asked.

Oh shit.

The king leans forward in his chair and unlike everything else in this place, it looks to be made of some smooth hard material that isn't dirt. Maybe because it's covered with goo that's seeping from the king's frame in buckets.

As he leans forward, strings of the goo form bridges between his body and the seat.

I'd barf if fear wasn't the thing filling my gut.

Bhihan's hands tighten on my ass almost possessively and I remind myself to act. So I lean into him and tuck my face into his neck, allowing myself enough room to send covert glances in the king's direction.

"You dare kill my kin and remain on the vessel on which you slaughtered him?" There is a hush that goes through the surrounding Darzel like a wave, and Bhihan tilts his head.

"You would have wanted nothing less than to meet the warrior who slaughtered your descendant."

Would he now?

It's hard for my eyes not to bug out and I have to grip on to Bhihan to release some of the tension through my fingers.

For a moment, the king does not respond. And then he huffs a grunt that reminds me of the warthog we may or may not meet very soon.

"You speak the truth." He huffs again and the crowd around us cheers. They frickin' cheer.

I lift my head slightly.

What?

They're rejoicing because we killed their prince? I don't get it.

"It is sorrowful that we did not get to see the slaughter firsthand."

"I agree," Bhihan says, but despite what seems to be a non-threatening mood from the king, Bhihan is rock solid. He's stiff, and I can feel the tension in his chest.

We're not out of the woods yet.

So I tuck my head against him again and do my best to look like the docile female he wants me to play.

"For that," the king says, "you cannot go unpunished."

Oh…here it comes. Dread fills me enough that I'm gripping the big alien so hard, he doesn't have to hold me up to keep me plastered to him.

"I must see the strength of the warrior who killed my kin. I must be satisfied his death was with honor," the king states.

Good thing they don't have video footage, because we pummeled him with a metal rod. Doubt they'd think that was honorable.

"You must enter the games. Give us a view of what we missed."

"So it will be."

I startle at that, lifting my head slightly as I gaze up at Bhihan. He agreed so easily.

The games. Those same games I saw that poor alien being slaughtered in. The death games, with the man-eating warthog.

I want to open my mouth and try to find another solution, but I can't. What other solution could I present?

I have to rely on the Atari I'm clutching on to. Opening my mouth will only make things worse for us.

The king sneers as he eyes us, and I sense when his gaze shifts to me. I can *feel* it.

"Take him to the cells. Leave the female here."

I stiffen and Bhihan goes solid underneath me.

"The female comes with me."

There is silence once again, and I swallow hard, tucking my face into his neck some more. "They'll kill me if you leave me here, won't they?"

I wonder if he hears my whisper. I doubt he'll answer me anyway, but his chin dips a fraction and low words only I can hear leave his lips.

"I'm positive they will."

I nod against him. Of course.

"The female is ours. We purchased her. She belongs to the Darzel— a much-awaited staple for our games."

I can't help but swallow hard a second time.

There has to be a way out of this.

But Bhihan only holds me tighter, a rumble going through his chest.

"She is mine. My mate. I won't be separated from her." I tilt my head so I can see his face. "Accept these terms or I will not fight."

Why is he doing this? Sticking out his neck for me?

Clearly, his species is known by these Darzel. Clearly, there is some sort of respect there, even if it may not have much weight in the current circumstances. And it seems, if I wasn't here, he might be able to negotiate his way out of this.

I stare at him, my gaze roving over his profile, trying to understand. But I can't.

Bhihan has no real reason to help me.

"Your *mate*?" the king inhales hard enough that a string of goo hanging from his nose goes up his nostril. "She does not carry your scent."

Bhihan bristles. I feel the movement go through his muscles like a wave.

"She has no mark." The king tilts his head and his attention makes a sliver of ice settle on my spine. "She is your mate?"

Bhihan's lips curl and his fangs make an appearance, albeit a slight one. As if he's trying to control his rising anger. "You insult me, king."

"If the female is not your mate—"

"She will have my scent before we leave this place," Bhihan speaks quickly. "Because we will leave this place. I'll win your games. I'll defeat your greatest monster. And then...you will set her free."

16

Bhihan

My female stiffens against me the moment the words leave my lips.

I can feel her stare, see through the corner of my eyes when her mouth falls open in shock.

The king grunts, a smile spreading his formless lips as he looks our way.

It's an offer he won't resist. An Atari warrior in his games and all he has to do is let a nameless female go free? It's a contract even the worst dealer could make.

The amount of entertainment I'll bring to his citizens, it's more than worth it. They will enjoy the death and the blood.

It's all the Darzel live for, anyway.

"Agreed," the king says. Not that I'm surprised. "Lead them to the dungeons. Give the Atari the best room." He stands, towering over his subjects, and I hold my little mate closer to me. "My fellow Darzel!" he proclaims. "Let the games begin!"

There is a roar from the surrounding Darzel and I hold back the urge to growl in annoyance.

As the Darzel lead us away, I have no doubt I can fulfill my part of this bargain. What worries me is what happens after I get this little female off this planet.

Will she make it to Atar?

I have no way of contacting the Zarzenius. She will be out there in the void on a craft all alone.

She has no home back on her planet, but she will find one on mine. And maybe, happiness. On Atar, she will be safe.

She is still looking at me. I can feel her gaze burning into my skin as strong as the star's rays that shine down on this planet. But I remind myself of my previous convictions.

I still have to make her hate me. That way, she can leave this place with no regrets. And most of all, without the weight of my mark on her skin.

I swallow hard, my fangs hurting as life spirit swells within them.

I'll need to release the pain somehow. Ease the pressure on my fangs, or it will drive me insane with the urge to mark her.

And I can't do that.

I can only think of one other way to make sure she has my scent and I am a thousand *marghuuls* sure that she will not like it.

My gaze finally slips down to hers as the Darzel following us chant.

Energy goes through them like a wave. They can't wait to see me fight. And I'll give them a show. I'll destroy their monsters, and I'll do it for her.

My female's brown eyes are filled with so many emotions I can't pinpoint just one. She stares at me unblinking, and as I look into her eyes, I know I am already mourning something that never was. That couldn't be.

I want to tell her everything will be fine. But the words that threaten my lips are the opposite. I want to say how sorry I am that she has been shackled with me. And…I wish I knew her name.

Wish I could whisper it, if even once, and explain it all.

But…possibly this is for the better.

She'd said I needed to earn the right to know her name. And she was right.

Only now, I am positive it will be a thing I might never know. Because this path I'm about to undertake, the path to make her hate me while guaranteeing her escape from this world, is a path on which I can only see us moving farther apart.

I lift a hand from her buttocks, and brush one of her braids from her face.

She doesn't wince or pull away. Probably still in shock. But her eyes remain on me, this time, her gaze telling me exactly what she is thinking.

She is puzzled by my actions. To her, it must make no sense at all.

The light suddenly dims as we enter a tunnel and most of the stream of Darzel at our back stay behind. Only a few follow us in and the one leading us grabs a torch from the wall as he makes his way down the walkway, the darkness growing deeper the farther we go.

It's cool down here, where the star's light does not shine.

The walkway tilts downward and we follow it deeper into the mountain of dirt until it levels out into a circular room.

My nostrils flare slightly as I look around at the array of cells in this space. All empty. No doubt the poor prisoners who once stayed here all died within days of arriving.

The Darzel who seems to be in charge approaches the largest cell and unlocks it, revealing a raised set of straw, a station to wash, and… nothing else.

"Your new home." He almost chitters with excitement and I scowl at him.

He backs away, giving me space to enter the room and as I walk in, I can almost feel the ghostly latch of shackles closing around my wrists.

I am a prisoner now…and so is she.

I turn with her in my arms, eyes on the few Darzel waiting outside the cell, and when they close it and still remain there watching, my lips curl.

A growl, more of a warning than anything else, grates against my throat and the Darzel startle.

"Leave."

They don't protest. Shuffling, they exit one behind the other. Leaving me in silence and with the one thing I've been trying to ignore since we landed on this cursed planet.

The female in my arms.

17

Bhihan

I set my female down. The fact that I'm referring to her as "my female" is not lost on me as her body disentangles from mine and rests on the raised surface for sleeping.

It is a strange feeling as I let her go. One that makes something ache inside me.

Loss. As if by letting her go, I am losing her and I realize immediately that it's the warmth and softness of her body that I'm already missing.

How?

How did I convince myself I didn't want this when this being is already making me question my sanity? My reservations. My whole reason for remaining on the Zarzenius avoiding females. Avoiding the one thing I was sure would rip me in two.

My female's gaze darts behind me and I can tell she's looking around to see if we're alone. As soon as she's satisfied, those far-too-intelligent eyes land on me.

"You're not really going to do this? Are you?"

What's that I hear in her voice? Concern?

"It's a death sentence. I've seen the monster they make you fight. It's not a normal beast. You can't be mad enough to volunteer to fight that thing."

Concern. Worry. For me. Why?

I want to lean into it, but that would be selfish of me.

She doesn't know she is my mate. And…she doesn't know that I am…

That you are what, Bhihan? Tempted to obey the fates. To feel what your brothers have experienced with their mates. To feel…wanted. Loved?

I growl at the thoughts in my head and, before me, her brows furrow.

"I don't…I don't understand you." Her throat moves and I have the urge to explain everything to her. But there is one thing I fear more than the thought of her hatred. And that is her rejection.

I may not know this female yet…but in another space, another time, I may have wanted to get to know her. And the thought of her rejecting me pierces me greater than anything else.

For hatred is still an emotion. It would mean, regardless that it's not love, my female feels something for me.

With rejection, she'd erase me completely.

It is a selfish thought.

A shameless one.

"You told the Darzel that you would fight if he sets me free." Her brown gaze searches mine and I cannot move. I stand here in her presence, knowing everything and knowing nothing. Wanting it all, and deserving none of it. I can only look at her. Soak in the promise of a matehood with her that I'll never have. "Why…why would you say such a thing?"

Her words pull me from my reverie and my head tilts, a furrow on my brow. "What do you mean?"

Her throat moves as she stares at me. The strength in her eyes, the rigidity of her shoulders as she grips the straw base beneath her. "Why did you say that you would fight for me?"

I…cannot reply. At the tip of my tongue, is everything I want to say to this female, but can't.

"You were joking, right? What's really your plan here?" When silence stretches between us, her jaw clenches. "Tell me. I may not be the best female to fight by your side. I may not be the strongest, the fittest, or the bravest. I may not be the most beautiful or the most helpful. And yes, I know I have lost one of my legs. You must see that as a great disability, especially in this situation. But I can help you."

She watches me, and all I can say is one word. "No."

"For fuck's sake." She curses underneath her breath, gripping the straw so hard, the tendons in her wrist stand out. "What do you want from me then? Why the hell would someone like you put themselves on the line for someone like me. You don't even know me. I mean *nothing* to you."

Ah…but that's where she is wrong. For in a matter of one night, she has come to mean *everything* to me.

"I may not be able to be the thing you need," I begin, something deep inside me aching when a sheen develops over her eyes. Eye waters. Tears. But not one drop falls. "I may not be the thing you need," I repeat, "but I will fight to the death so you can leave this place."

"But *why*?"

"That…is something you might discover when you get to Atar. You will be safe there. A new life awaits."

Mona

The Atari turns and sits on the floor, resting his back against the corner of the cage. I can only stare at him as he does.

None of this makes sense.

Generosity comes with a price. And this alien is giving me the most generous gift that anyone has ever bestowed on me…and for nothing?

There must be a catch.

And if he thinks he is going to go out in that ring and fight, get himself killed on my behalf, he is mistaken.

To live with that knowledge would probably tear me apart.

Not that I expect him to really do it.

When they come for him, I'll see what his true intentions are. Maybe he will make a run for it, leave me here to rot in this cell. Or maybe he will throw me to the wolves.

Either way, I'll be prepared.

But as I watch him, his words echo in my mind. Nothing he said paints him as a man that will go against his word. It's almost like I can trust him with this too…and that's a scary thought.

For a stranger to give up his life for me…

Shit like that only happens in the holo novels I sometimes found on my clean-up runs on Lower Earth.

That stuff doesn't happen in real life.

Reality, *my* reality, is filled with pain and hard work. There is no love. No one to count on. It's a cold, cruel world that I have to survive in until it's my time to go. And even thinking about that now, I wonder why I keep on fighting. What makes me wake up and press on?

The Atari releases a breath and his eyes close, but I know he's not sleeping.

He probably just doesn't want to speak to me.

He confuses me. I don't know whether to be angry at him or to think of him as a friend. Everything that he's done so far point to the latter, but it almost feels as if there's something I'm missing. And it's that feeling that holds me rigid. Aware of his every move. Expecting that something unfortunate will happen at any moment. That he'll show me his true colors and I'll be right all along.

Rising, I balance on my leg as I hop toward the bars, grasping them for support as I look outside the cell.

I can feel his eyes on me the moment I move but I try not to pay him any attention. I get the sense he wants some time to think and who wouldn't?

He must be realizing exactly what he said out there. The promise he made.

He watches me as I move around the cell, holding on to the bars as I make my way.

The bars are made of the same material I suppose made the king's chair.

It's not metal but it's not wood either.

It's hard though. Hard enough that trying to hit it with my hand and bend or break it is futile.

"It's *nesha*." The Atari's deep voice fills the room. "That material reacts to the energy you exert upon it, pushing back with equal force."

I stop gripping the bars so tight. "So, I'm basically fighting myself. There's no way to break it and get out."

When I look at him, there's a sadness in those golden eyes that makes me pause.

He shakes his head before pulling his gaze from mine and something deep inside me …reacts.

I don't know what sort of reaction this is. It's pain. Pain other than the type I'm used to feeling.

There's an urge to move over to the big alien and discover what's wrong.

I give myself a mental shake. When did I become so caring?

And yet…the urge is still there.

To reach out.

Turning, I let gravity carry me as I fall onto the straw bed. My face is turned his way and I find him watching me.

We stare at each other. His gaze locked with mine, and it feels like I'm watching a world move behind his eyes. A world as complicated as mine. A world filled with as much hidden pain and torment as mine.

I can't pull my gaze away, and he doesn't look away either.

We stay like that, gazing at each other as the seconds tick by, until I forget I'm in a cell, locked away underneath a mountain, waiting for the end.

All I can see is him and all the thoughts expressed in those eyes.

Pain.

Want.

Hope.

Longing.

Such deep longing.

What I see in Bhihan's eyes terrifies me…because it's everything I have felt but never ever said out loud.

Love. A partner.

A *home*.

The vivid thoughts in his eyes scare me. Because they paint a picture of everything I want and everything I'll never have.

Mona

I wake with a start, partially horrified I'd fallen asleep and a bit out of sorts, sleep still making me drowsy.

My eyes fly open to lock with golden ones and I surprise myself by not jerking away. Instead, a comforting feeling engulfs me at the sight of the Atari.

He's close, almost as if he was about to kiss me, and memory of that kiss we shared on the ship comes rushing back.

He lied to them that I'm his mate.

That's one thing I need to bring up with him.

"What are you doing?" My voice is soft, almost a whisper, and his lashes dip as his gaze falls to my lips.

They're long, white like the hair on his head, and complement the gold in his eyes.

"Checking if you were breathing," he says, his voice low, matching the pitch of mine.

A soft smile tugs the corner of my lips. "Won't get rid of me so easily, I'm afraid."

"I don't want to."

My smile freezes as a lump forms in my throat. And that's when I notice he isn't wearing his space suit anymore.

He's removed it, and before me now, is a male dressed only in dark leather-like trousers.

A hard sculpted chest is right before me, the scent of forest rain rushing into my nostrils as soon as I breathe in.

"Sometimes, I wonder if you're my friend or—"

"Your foe? If you should trust me...hate me..."

My eyes narrow slightly. "Hate is a strong word."

"Aye...but some things are necessary."

I frown. He's still close. Hasn't moved since I opened my eyes to find him there.

"Why are you whispering?"

He turns his head slightly, his gaze focusing on something outside the bars and that's when I finally turn and look, alarm going through me the moment my eyes land on the group of Darzel standing there. Watching us.

The hairs stand up along my arms, a spike of something sour going straight to my gut.

The Darzel king is there with his minions. His eyes glued on us as if he's watching strange animals in an exhibit.

My heart thumps as my eyes fly back to Bhihan.

"It is time for me to go," he says, and my heart does a flailing thump once more.

No. Not yet. I haven't come up with a plan yet.

But wait...

I watch as he rises, slowly turning from me, and my eyes widen.

He's really going to do it?

He takes the few steps it takes to close the distance between him and the cell bars, and it's all moving too fast. Too quickly.

He's really doing it. He's not planning on running away? Leaving me here?

"Secure the Atari," the king speaks and I know that at this moment, as I watch the Atari leave the cell, it might be the last time I see him alive.

"Wait!"

They all freeze and my heart thumps as I try to rise quickly, bracing on my arms so I can stand. But the tremors going through me make balancing hard and I slip, falling on my ass.

"Bhihan!"

I try to rise again when strong arms support mine and I look up into the face of the Atari. He's returned to my side, concern flooding his gaze.

"Are you hurt?"

I blink at him, my eyes darting to the Darzel still watching us.

There is no privacy. So I do the one thing I can think of.

Arms circling his shoulders, I palm the back of his neck, pulling him closer to me. A rumble goes through him but he relents, coming closer even as a shiver goes through his frame.

Placing my face on the side of his that's away from the attention of the Darzel, I brush my lips over his neck, moving up to his ear.

Bhihan trembles, a slight groan leaving his lips.

"Kiss me, Bhihan."

He stiffens before he relents, almost as if whatever war he's fighting within him was easily lost.

His lips close over the skin at my shoulder and my eyelids flutter with the warmth of his mouth.

We're only pretending. This isn't real.

I have to remind myself, even as a pulse goes through my core.

"You can't go out there," I whisper as my lips brush against his ear.

Wrapping my arms around him tighter, I hope to the Darzel, we simply look like two lovebirds that can't get enough of each other.

The skin at the nape of his neck is thicker and hotter than I expect, and as I pull him closer, it pulses under my fingers.

"You can't go out there. You'll die."

He shifts, changing position as he forces my head back, his tongue following a path across my clavicle around to the other side of my head.

Now it's my turn to see the Darzel watching us with almost greedy eyes, and a shudder goes through me.

"You have no faith in me." Bhihan's deep voice feels like it vibrates in my ear, sending another pulse through to my core.

I don't know how long I'm going to be able to put up with this fake relationship thing. For years, no man has stirred any real feelings within me. And yet this stranger who doesn't even know my name is making me react without even trying to.

Maybe because with him, there are no expectations. I know exactly what he wants, and that's to get out of this mess. The same thing that I want. He's "using" me, with my consent. The same as I am using him.

"I promise you, my female," he speaks louder, loud enough that I know the Darzel can hear and I almost see their ears perk as they listen, "I'll come back to you bearing the blood of my enemies. You need not worry about me."

I swallow hard, clutching on to him a little too long before he pulls away. And when he stands and looks down at me, I wish I could read the thoughts behind his eyes.

There's a distinct resignation there now, one I have often worn myself.

Turning, he heads toward the cell door as it opens to let him through, and as he passes the Darzel king, if I had a throwing knife I would sail it through the air and right into the fiend's sneering mouth.

As Bhihan disappears from the room, several Darzel guarding him, the king turns to look at me and my eyes narrow. A distinct cold brushes over my skin as I stare into this king's beady eyes.

His arms move, bridges of goo extending from his torso as he gestures, almost theatrically slowly, for me to follow in Bhihan's path.

Another lump forms in my throat as we stare at each other. Me against the king.

He wants me to follow Bhihan. Why?

"As a…*guest* of the Darzel…you must watch the games too."

I pull in air through my nostrils slowly, willing myself to remain calm. To think clearly. To not overreact.

"I'll watch." I square my eyes with his. He will smell no fear from me. Because of all the things in this known universe, there is only one thing I am truly afraid of, and it's not him. "But I need a walking aid."

I narrow my eyes slightly, waiting for his response.

He says nothing. The only thing that makes me aware he has heard my request is that the same arm that gestured that I could leave the cell signs some kind of command and a Darzel scurries away.

As we remain watching each other, sizing each other up, there's a clang as something is thrown into the cell.

It looks like a stick, but I quickly realize it's made of the same material that makes the bars. With a slight curve on one end, I reckon it reaches up to my shoulder.

Reaching for it, I brace on it as I stand, wishing I had those cargo pants I usually wore to work. They had pockets so deep I'd occasionally lose my tools, but they were great at hiding shit I could use to defend myself.

Gripping the makeshift walking stick, I put pressure on it. It's thin, but it bears my weight as I move forward, using it like a crutch. If anything happens, it will have to be my weapon of choice, and as I near the Darzel, my fingers almost itch as I watch them with wary eyes.

If they try anything…

But they don't.

The king turns away from me as soon as I reach the entrance of the cell and follows in the direction Bhihan had gone.

I follow behind him, aware of the several Darzel coming up at my back, and brace for anything out of the ordinary.

We walk through a winding path that may be the same as the one we followed down to the cells, or not. I'm not sure.

This place is like an ant's nest with connecting tunnels and soon, we reach a bigger area that branches out again.

Distantly, I hear sounds. Cheering. Roaring. And my heartbeat picks up.

Bhihan.

The king disappears, moving up an incline where I can see the sun's rays like a blinding light at the top. I move to follow him when a Darzel blocks my path, coming close enough, his gooey skin almost touches mine.

I stop short as he gestures in a separate direction. An offshoot to the incline, but one where I can see light anyway.

As the Darzel heads that way, leading me down the offshoot, I glance behind me. There is only one in front of me and one guarding the back. I can take them if need be. I'd have to.

My eyes falls to their strange feet. They have flat pads over their soles that extend almost to their ankles. Like strange built-in boots, it protects their feet from the dirt and, in effect, protects the dirt from their goo.

If this crutch fails me and I have to remove my boot to clobber one of these green assholes, at least I won't have to worry about getting poisoned through my foot.

I keep this in mind as the cheering and noise from outside sounds louder the closer we get to the light and soon, we are in a small room.

There are bars right in front of me. Short ones about the length of my arm, and the Darzel give me space as I move toward them.

I can see outside. The exact arena that I'd seen in the holo vid greats my eyes. But we're below ground level. The bottom of the bars rests into the earth and as I come to stand in front of them, only my face would be visible on the other side.

I scour what I can see of the arena but Bhihan is nowhere in sight.

Then, there is a deafening roar.

My heart rises in my throat as I step even closer, bracing on my crutch so I can stand on tiptoe to see better.

I have never been more afraid for someone else in my life. And I tell myself it's illogical, that I shouldn't care. I should be happy that he's saying he'll fight to the death so I can go free. It's his life, right?

But even with the ice I've packed around my heart for what feels like centuries, I can't harbor such thoughts.

This male is going to go there to fight a monster. And all for what? Because he saw my sorry ass hanging off a ship, desperate to escape the very beings we're now in the clutches of.

Shit.

The roaring only seems to get louder and my eyes widen, searching the huge arena for the large figure of my Atari warrior. But I still can't see him.

I realize shortly after, the cheering is for the arrival of the Darzel king.

He appears on a throne-like platform separated from his people.

Directly across from me, and far enough that I can't see his features clearly, sight of him as he sits and looks in my direction shouldn't have the hairs on the back of my neck rising.

They do anyway.

The cheering dies down as he raises a gooey hand and for moments, all I can hear is the sound of my own breathing. But for the life of me, I can't quell the terror starting to shoot through my veins.

The king waves a hand, and the arena erupts. Even the Darzel guarding me rush toward the bars, one on either side. But they are too short to see outside. I see them eyeing me for a few moments, and it's clear guarding me isn't a job they'd pick if they had the choice. But I ignore them, my eyes glued on the outside, desperate for a glimpse of him.

And then I see him. The moment Bhihan appears is the moment the crowd becomes almost deafening.

They rise in the stands and scream their lungs out as he walks to the center of the arena.

I grip the bars tighter, my wide eyes on him as he comes to a stop.

Bronze skin glistens under the sun as he faces the king, head high, shoulders broad, not an ounce of fear radiating from his being.

The king raises a hand, and the crowd dies with surprising obedience.

"Warrior of Atar! You come to pay a debt!"

The crowd is still hushed and the king's words carry across the still air.

"Release the quigar!"

I could not grip the bars tighter even if I tried.

Shouts and cheers erupt in the crowd as, in what looks like a dark tunnel below where the king sits, a loud grating sound pierces through the air as if bars are being pulled.

What follows after is a roar that chills me to my bones.

I'm dimly aware of the Darzel guarding me cursing in Galactic Standard before they disappear from the room, probably to get a better vantage point so they can watch the match.

I'm alone now. I could make a run for it maybe, but I can't bring myself to move.

And as I stand there staring, a roar bellows through the air, hitting me full-on as if I was right beside the animal.

Something thumps. Something big. Big enough for the earth to shake and I watch as Bhihan crouches slightly, planting his feet into the earth.

From somewhere in the crowd, something falls and clangs in the dirt near him. A sword and I wonder why he doesn't rush to take it.

I see why shortly after.

There, from the dark tunnel, a face appears.

Pitch black and with scales that look like they belong on a dragon, the biggest cat I've ever seen in my life stalks out of the tunnel.

It looks around, twisting its head as it takes in the crowd. Sharp fangs bare as it roars once more, slamming down its front paws into the earth.

A billow of dust hides it for a moment.

It's the size of a hovercar and has scales that look impenetrable. Now I understand why Bhihan didn't move to take up the sword. He knew what the animal was even before I did.

And as the quigar finally turns and spots him standing there, waiting for it, it pauses, crouching just like a cat would when it sees prey.

As it stares at my Atari, it's like the beast is looking directly at me, and my heart aches and pants, erratic beats overcoming me to the point I cannot breathe.

Gripping the bars I say the first prayer I've said since that time when I was nine years old.

I pray he survives this.

I pray he lives.

19

Bhihan

The quigar is a beast most hunters fear.

Sharp claws. Sharp teeth. Fangs that will rip your innards out. And a natural armor that is impenetrable.

There is only one way to defeat a quigar.

And I know how.

As the beast charges at me, that sensitive skin at my neck pulses as I jump, taking myself out of the way of its charge and causing it to skid in the dirt.

But my skin isn't pulsing because of the danger before me. It's pulsing because my mate touched me there. Pulled me to her. Told me to put my lips on her skin even while hers brushed against my ear, her husky voice speaking to me. Making me want.

My skin pulses because she touched me there, the most sensitive spot on any Atari apart from his cock, and she told me she cared.

Not in so many words. No, my female doesn't show weakness in that way. I know that now.

As the quigar shakes its backside, getting ready to charge at me again, the Darzel crowd cheers.

I ready myself once more, waiting until it moves, and that's when I see her.

I don't know how I spot her through that narrow little view box that's barely visible, but I do.

I feel her eyes on me and even from this distance, I can sense her distress.

It warms something deep.

I'd wondered whether she'd care. Whether she'd take my offer to fight for her without ever looking back.

I told myself she should. That it's what a male like me deserves.

But another part, the same part that's finding it so hard making the little female hate me, even though I've decided she should, that same part wished that she would…care.

And seeing her there tells me she does.

As the quigar darts at me, I know not whether the Darzel crowd cheers for me or to see the quigar rip me apart. Probably the latter. They live for blood and gore. But my mate, she doesn't cheer.

She grips the bars tighter, almost as if she can't bear to see me harmed.

And somehow, I grasp that feeling and I tuck it somewhere deep inside me where no one will ever be able to take it away.

I hang on to it as I slide to the side, spinning as the quigar misses and charges right past me, the shouts and cheers in the Darzel crowd mere background noise to my focus.

I am doing this for her.

The quigar skids to a halt and looks at me over its shoulder.

Unlike most beasts, it's not mindless, and as I look into its eyes, I see when it realizes I'm not some silly, easy-to-catch prey.

It will change its tactic now. Be more strategic. And that is the very reason I did not grasp the sword that was thrown down to me.

If I had, the quigar would have taken me as a warrior ready to kill it as soon as it advanced. It would not have attacked thinking I was easy to get rid of. And in that one simple thing, I found its weakness.

As it turns and studies me, its tail rising in the air behind it, I smile.

"You made a mistake, quigar, rushing at me like that." I stand tall, taking a few measured steps as we begin to stalk each other in a circle. "You forgot your defenses, thinking I was an easy kill."

Because anyone who knows anything about beasts would know one thing about quigars. Each is born with a sensitive spot on one leg. A spot that, if pierced, will render that leg useless.

Finding which leg holds the spot is the tricky bit, for, with its rising intelligence, quigars have adapted to hide their disability.

Their weak spot is often not discovered until it's too late.

Still smiling, I grab the sword from the dirt and the quigar's ears perk. Then it snarls, sharp fangs baring as its lips pull back.

I am ready when it comes at me and I launch myself in the air, somersaulting as I turn my head in the direction of my mate.

She is still there. Watching. And it gives me purpose.

I catch her face for only a moment before I land on the other side of the quigar.

The beast stops short, expecting my fall but I am too fast. I roll, thrusting the sword upright as I slide through the dirt, the sharp end of the weapon burying into the beast's flesh, cutting a path that makes its life blood spray as I attack the very spot that will give me an upper hand. The beast roars, spinning suddenly and with a force that throws me several meters away.

I tumble, dust billowing and for a moment, I wonder if my plan didn't work. But when something thumps to the earth so hard, the ground shakes, I know I made the right decision.

Getting to my feet, I see the quigar desperately trying to stand, but its leg does not respond. It's left with only one option, to come at me with only the remaining three. But it's slow now, and I am faster.

I see the fear in its eyes as I charge at it, leaping into the air as it swipes at me. I land at its wounded leg, pulling the sword from its flesh as it roars again in pain. It swipes at me again, claws wanting blood, and I swing the sword, sliding through its flesh once more.

Its lifeblood paints me in dark red and the Darzel go wild.

They want to see me cut the creature and as the quigar whimpers, trying to crawl back to the hole they released it from, I almost have second thoughts.

But this is not for me. This is for her.

I can have no mercy while her life hangs in the balance.

My female. The one who must live.

In those days where she will live on, I wish I could be around to get to know exactly who she is. But I'll settle for knowing that she is alive on Atar.

Right now, that is all that matters.

20

Mona

He did it.

He actually single-handedly did it.

The crowd goes wild. I swear some of them are frothing in the stands as they watch Bhihan gut the poor animal. It collapses at his feet and he turns in a slow circle.

I expect him to raise his hands and accept the Darzel's praise, but all he does is turn till he is looking in my direction.

Back turned to the king, my Atari looks at *me*.

"Bhihan," I whisper his name as he lets the sword fall from his hands.

The crowd erupts even more as he exits the arena, and I brace on the crutch, making haste as I turn and head out of the room.

Two Darzel, the ones I assume are guarding me, appear and lead me back to the cell and as I step inside it, I can't help but pace.

Minutes go by and Bhihan doesn't return.

My heart is in my chest by the time I hear sounds coming from one of the corridors. Spinning, I turn in that direction, standing still in the center of the cell while my heart continues to pound in my chest.

The moment he enters the room, he pauses and we stand looking at each other before I find myself moving.

I hurry to the open cell door, and I know I'm wearing my emotions on my face. But I can't seem to school my features. To hide my panic or the fact that I...*care.*

I care about this male. About the fact he just went out there and fought a monster for me. And that he's done this without me asking.

I didn't need to beg.

I didn't need to bargain.

As he starts walking again, I stop just before the entrance of the cell, tracking him with my eyes, and when he steps inside, the Darzel slam the cell door shut behind him, causing an almost deafening clang to echo in the small space.

But I don't budge. I don't wince. I cannot move.

I can only look at him.

And the moment the Darzel shuffle out of the room, I close the distance.

I don't know what I'm doing, or why, but I brace on the crutch with one arm and lift the other. My fingers hover over his skin.

He looks uninjured. But now that I am close to him, I can see the small scrapes across his skin from tumbling with that monster outside.

"Do," I gulp, "Do these hurt?"

My fingers move like a ghost across his chest as I lift my eyes, spotting even more of the tiny scrapes running up across his shoulder.

My hand trembles.

Why is seeing these minor cuts dissolving the effect of my resolve? No. *Where* has my resolve gone? Why am I feeling a lump of pain in my chest for this male?

The answer comes immediately. Like an arrow shooting into my brain. Because...of all the people I've encountered in my life, this male has yet to demand anything of me. This Atari has only given.

But what happens when he does end up demanding something?

I bite back the ache that comes with that question, releasing a slow breath as I let my fingers settle on his skin.

A ripple goes through his frame, but otherwise, he stands still, watching me, gazing down at me with unreadable eyes.

"Do they hurt?" I repeat, locking eyes with him this time.

His throat moves and a moment passes between us.

Memory of his lips, his tongue against mine makes a flutter go through my belly. And even though I know we kissed because of the fake relationship, pushing away that flutter only makes it stronger.

Whatever happens by the end of this, I'll be a total wreck.

But right now…staring into this Atari's eyes…time stops.

My hand slips up higher, reaching the nape of his neck and I can't stop myself from leaning forward.

But the moment is interrupted. Broken the second he grasps my wrist and pulls my hand away from his skin.

That flutter in my belly stops immediately, but the frantic beats of my heart lag behind.

"Don't," is all he says, and I blink several times, trying to catch my bearings.

Right.

Only when there's an audience.

Was I really just about to kiss him?

Shame and embarrassment make me turn, ready to move away from him, the walls I built years before adding another layer, crumpling the newfound bridges that were beginning to form.

But as I attempt to pull away, Bhihan's hand tightens on my wrist as he yanks on my arm.

The sudden movement makes me lose hold of my crutch and it falls with a clang as his lips descend on mine.

The protest, those words of denial that were beginning to spout on my tongue, die the moment we kiss.

Bhihan pulls me to him, supporting me against him as his lips press against mine, his tongue moving against mine as a whimper I had no time to hold back escapes my chest.

He groans. Hard enough that I feel the vibration as his hand dips, moving to grasp my butt as he pulls me flush against him.

The hardness underneath his trou presses into my belly as his kiss deepens. And at the moment when my eyes are about to close, I hear a voice that puts everything into focus.

"Well done, Atari."

The Darzel king enters the room and it all suddenly makes sense.

My heart drops. I'm such a fool.

As Bhihan releases me, turning so he can face the Darzel king, I pick up the shattered pieces of my pride and stoop to grab my crutch that had fallen.

I hardly hear what they speak about. Their words become mumbling that my mind doesn't care to focus on. All that is center-most in my thoughts is the fact that I am open. Bare.

Vulnerable.

What's happening to me?

What's this pain in my chest that's so different from the pain I'm so used to?

This hurts more. I can already feel it.

And what's scary is I can feel its propensity to destroy me.

As I rise with the crutch balanced underneath my arm, stray words finally penetrate my consciousness.

"...still have not marked her. Is she really your mate, Atari...or are you trying to trick me."

I can hardly see around Bhihan. Somehow, he seems even bigger and more imposing than before. But the Darzel that I can see all have their eyes on me.

Those dark beady eyes glisten like obsidian jewels as they stare at me and I don't have to take note of the hairs rising all along my arms to understand that I am in danger.

Why are they looking at me? Bhihan just gave them what they wanted. Blood. Death. Gore.

"She is mine."

He says the words so easily. Almost as if he believes them. But I guess I am the fool. The one mixing reality with fantasy. The one who is going against everything she's ever told herself.

But this is survival, and I've always survived. No matter what it takes.

So I move to his side and I hold my chin tall. I meet the king's eyes, unflinching.

"I am his."

Bhihan stiffens at my side, a rumble in his chest that I don't know the meaning of. But the Darzel king does. For even in beady eyes, a flicker of emotion shines through.

Interest.

Curiosity.

"Prove it."

I stiffen. Prove it?

We kissed. I've practically melted in Bhihan's arms. What more proof does this asshole need?

"Mate her now."

My mouth falls open as I stare at the king. What?

"Seed your mate. Meld your scents. Fill her ripe belly with your kits."

"Wh-what?"

My wide eyes fly to Bhihan and I'm even more horrified he doesn't look as shocked as I do.

His gaze narrows on the Darzel king and a few beats pass where I could cut the air with a knife if I had one.

"So she is *not* your mate..." The king takes a step forward. "Then she will enter the games."

My heart stops in my throat and, as if he knows, the king's beady eyes twinkle on me.

I can see my reflection in those eyes. And my death.

I see myself being ripped apart in that arena, disemboweled by one of those monsters.

I'd thought the warthog monster was the only one. But it's clear I was wrong.

Just which creature is he imagining taking my life?

I can see the glee in his eyes. Sense that's exactly what he's imagining. And my shoulders stiffen as my lips curl.

I step forward and I can feel Bhihan as he turns, his eyes landing on me.

"You want me to fight?" My chest heaves as I face the king face to face. "You want to see me out there with one of your monsters?"

"You will..." His head dips and I can sense the devil living in him. He's not the king only because he's the biggest of these fuckers. He's different from the others. Those Darzel that bought me, the same ones I helped kill, didn't give me this feeling.

This feeling of being in the presence of some great evil.

And he is evil.

Which being would not mourn the death of his own child, but instead order the one that killed him to fight some more just so he could watch.

It's despicable and the thought only makes my lips curl some more.

"Fine," I say.

There's no going around this.

Whether I like it or not, I'm going to end up out there in that arena, fighting for my life, and I rather it be my decision—or at least, as much of my decision as it can be—rather than some fiend's orders that send me out there to my death.

"I'll fight."

There are chitters of excitement from the other Darzel now, also no doubt imagining my demise, and for the first time, I see the king smile.

His teeth are sharp. Carnivorous. And for a moment, my bravado fails as my heart thumps with distress. But I push past it.

"I'll fight. But you have to let him go free first." I jerk my thumb in Bhihan's direction.

Yes, I might be hurt by the confusing emotions this whole ordeal has awakened within me, but I'm not heartless. And even though this whole fake relationship thing has thrown me out of my element, I'm still sane enough to know that Bhihan doesn't belong here.

If not for me, he would still be safe on his ship.

"Let him go, and I'll give you the best show of your life."

Or, at least, I'll try.

"I would rather die first." Bhihan grabs me by the arm, enough to make my body turn toward him.

His eyes are a blazing fire of rage and disbelief.

"What do you think you're doing?!" he hisses.

"Trying to save you." I jerk against his arm.

"Aye. But I don't need to be saved. You are my mate. I am meant to protect you from all harm."

I close my eyes tight for a moment. Enough with this mate thing. The king already sees right through us.

I open my eyes to say just this when Bhihan turns his rage in the king's direction.

"She is mine. You wish to be sure? I will mate with her now."

My eyelids flutter a thousand times. What?

My mouth hangs open in shock as Bhihan turns and scoops me into his arms. Eyes wide, I can only stare at him.

"What are you doing?" My harsh whisper does nothing to draw his attention as he seems purely focused on taking me to the straw bed. As he sets me down, I can only stare up at him.

He reaches to his waist and pulls on his trou, discarding it somewhere else in the cage.

Is he…wait…this is happening too fast. He can't be serious.

My heart lurches as my gaze falls down his frame, to land on the massive cock staring back at me.

He's hard. So so hard. And big.

And the throb that goes straight down to my center is one I can't ignore.

I groan. I'm helpless.

But this isn't right.

Bhihan palms his cock, the look in his eyes growing heated as he looks down at me.

"Leave," he growls.

"Atari—"

"I won't mate my female in your presence! Leave. When you return by the next day, you will know that she is mine. And I will fight again."

He looks over his shoulder at the king, his eyes like a furnace of rage, and in my peripheral vision, I see the Darzel slowly leaving the room.

"Very well, Atari."

I'm frickin' surprised the king acquiesces, but I can only lie there on my back, completely frozen as I stare at Bhihan.

When the room empties and it's just us two, I think he will relax his shoulders and put his trou back on. We will have to find another way to trick the king or do what he says. But Bhihan doesn't get dressed. Instead, that smoldering gaze moves back to me.

"Bhihan?"

Why's my voice trembling? Why is my *heart* trembling? Why can't I pull my eyes away from the sight of his dick? And why is there a rhythmic thrum going through my lady bits?

"Remove the tunic."

His words are barely more than a growl and I stare at him, confused.

"You can't be serio—"

He leans forward, releasing his hold on his cock as he crawls over me on all fours till we are face to face.

My breath hitches in my throat.

"You are beautiful," he breathes. "So beautiful. Any male would be honored for you to be their mate."

My brows furrow slightly. What's happening?

"We must do this. Your safety is non-negotiable."

I swallow hard, forcing past the lump of emotions rising in my throat. "You want us to have sex…"

"More than anything," he groans. "More than qeffing anything…"

Okay.

Wait. What?

That bud between my folds swells and pulses at his words.

"…but this is not the way I want to have you." He shifts and his cock slaps against my belly, sending another pulse through my slit.

"If you will allow…" He pauses, his eyes dipping to my lips as a breath shudders from his chest. "If you allow me to coat you with my spend, it will have the same effect. You will smell as if I claimed you. The Darzel won't know the difference."

I swallow hard again. "Coat me?"

I know exactly what he means but I can't believe any of this is happening. I'm in a state of shock and want. No. Need.

That throbbing between my legs grows insistent the longer he remains close. And it's confusing because I'm sure it shouldn't be happening.

"I'll release on you." Bhihan meets my gaze, and every word he says makes tingles go through me. "You will smell the way you should. Like you're mine."

I gulp again, eyes locked with his as I search for the lies I often see in others. But there are none. All I see is heat. Heat that I want to engulf me.

Hesitantly, I nod, and his eyes roll back for a moment, his cock jerking between us, hard enough that it pokes into my belly.

I bite my lip, knowing I'm going down a road I can never return from.

Because a part of me wants more than he is offering.

And want is the enemy of happiness.

Like a landslide, I'm falling for this male.

And I...I can't seem to stop.

But everyone knows landslides only bring pain and destruction. Will I even be whole in the end?

21

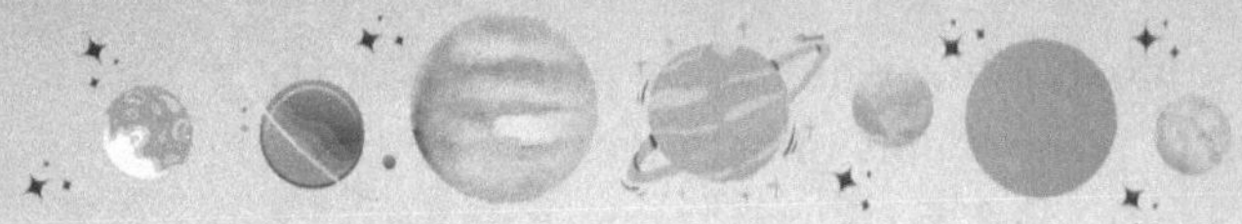

Mona

I try to measure my breaths as I lift my arms and shrug out of the tunic. A shiver goes through me even though the room is warm, but I can't seem to steady my racing heart.

Bhihan watches my every movement, and though I know we won't do the deed, it feels strange just lying here like a board. I suppose I can help him.

So I take my clothes off, underwear and all. He even reaches down and helps me to remove my boot, and then we are nude together. Bare before each other. Nothing to hide behind.

It's not like when we were skin-to-skin on the ship. This is different.

There is a tension here circling us that makes every nerve ending on my skin stand at attention. Every breath we take. Every slight movement.

Even his gaze. That heated gaze that moves slowly across my skin as if he's soaking in every detail.

There are tingles all across my skin and an ache growing between my thighs the longer he stares at me, and when I think I can't take it anymore, Bhihan eases back on his haunches.

His thick cock bounces and slaps against his pelvis with such strength, I ache at the thought of what it would feel like buried within me.

I gulp back a needy whimper, half embarrassed by my reaction, fully mortified by what's happening to my body.

I've never reacted to a male like this before. Never.

I don't know what's happening to me...and what's worse, I don't know if I hate it either.

Bhihan releases the sexiest grunt as he grasps himself at the base, stroking gently.

He hasn't even started yet, and that one action is so hot, I swallow hard.

I can't pull my eyes away from what he's doing as he massages his base, a long bead of pre-cum forming at his flared tip and rolling down the ridges to hang off like a string beckoning me to catch it with my tongue.

I want to taste it and the urge is sudden, so strong, that I am momentarily arrested by it. So I catch my bottom lip, pulling the flesh into my mouth as I bite down hard. The pain brings me some focus, forcing my mind to clear. But it does nothing to the ache growing between my thighs.

I lick my lips and Bhihan groans suddenly, his wrist halting its movement. Flicking my gaze to his face, my chest heaves as I stare at the fire there. The *need*.

"I...I can help." I can hardly get the words out. "I can help you."

I ease up on my elbows, ready to scoot forward and give him some assistance. After all, once again, he's having to do something for *my* benefit, but his growl holds me still.

"Don't. If you touch me right now..."

My mouth goes dry, my heart thumping as I look at him, aware that he gives his cock some long slow strokes as he meets my eyes.

But I nod. "If it will interrupt you—"

"Interrupt me?" His hand pauses for a moment as he leans closer, closer still, close enough that his face is so near to mine, I can feel his breath on my lips.

And I can't move. I don't want to.

"If you touch me, I cannot promise I won't pin you down and mate with you. But this is not…it is not what you deserve."

What I deserve?

His words are touching and confusing at the same time and my breath hitches as he suddenly eases back, his fist pumping harder as he brings his palm up over his ridges, squeezing right under the tip before stroking once again.

I fall back, hands digging into the tightened straw as I watch him.

It's not even what he's doing to his cock anymore. It's the look in his eyes. As if he wants to devour me.

My hands move all on their own, one closing around a boob as the other moves to my center. And the moment I touch myself, Bhihan freezes. His chest heaves as he looks at me for a few moments, and something, I don't know what it is, maybe it's the look in his eyes that drives me crazy, but I whimper as I dip my fingers between my folds, my eyelids fluttering at the jolt of pleasure my body has been begging for.

A groan rumbles through his chest as his fingers tighten around his shaft and he gives himself one hard pump, his eyes glued on my fingers before they move to my face.

"You tempt me, my mate."

His mate.

The words sounds so good.

To be someone's mate. Their all. The perfect other half.

A thing like that's too unbelievable for me. But I soak in the word anyway. I let it warm me as I whimper, adding another finger as I swirl them over that heated bud at the center of my folds.

Bhihan groans and I whimper, my eyes fluttering open enough to watch as he strokes himself.

He's watching me. Watching my every movement. The way my fingers move and I bite my lips. The way my chest rises and falls. The way I pant, my breaths increasing as I pinch my nipple. And I watch him too.

The way his chest heaves as he breathes, rising and falling with the rhythm of his fist. The way he's looking at me as if I'm the most beautiful, sexiest thing he's ever laid eyes on. And the way his fangs descend over his lips, the tips dripping as if he could bite into me if he could. The thought almost makes me come.

I'm close and my eyes roll back, a whimper going through me.

"I dishonor you, my mate."

My eyes fall on him and he shudders, his cock pulsing in his hand.

"How?" I whisper. "What do you mean?" And why is he still calling me his mate even now? There's no one here watching us. We have no audience. It's just him and me.

No smoke barriers. No hidden tactics.

Just us.

"To spray my spend on your skin and not inside your tight warmth...I..."

A lump in my throat makes me swallow hard even as a pulse goes through my center.

"I have failed you."

I shake my head. That's furthest from the truth. But he continues.

"Will you accept this? Me? My spend?"

I nod, my throat going so dry again that I have to swallow once more. I *want* him to do it.

"Even though I've not yet earned the right to know your name?"

I don't know why his words make tears gather at the corner of my eyes. He took that so seriously?

"Mona," I croak. "My name's Mona. Ramona of Earth, but I want you to call me by the new name I gave myself. Mona."

He blinks at me, his throat moving as his cock twitches in his hand as if it's ready to burst.

"Mona," he groans. "My mate, Mona."

His words make my eyelids flutter and I lean back fully, opening myself to him.

"Please," I whisper.

And Bhihan grunts.

His cock twitches as streams of cum shoot from his flared tip, coating my leg, my belly, my breasts. And it keeps coming.

As I look down my body at him, fear of my past rears its head and, for a moment, I wonder if I'll see the conquest in his eyes.

But all I see is Bhihan gazing at me as he covers me in his cum. Obsession in his eyes.

And I latch on to that look like it's a drug.

Because it's exactly what I want.

No.

It's what I *need*.

22

My mate is the most beautiful being in existence. Lying in front of me, covered in my spend, there is no greater image.

I try to capture the moment, burning her image into my mind, because I know I may never see her like this again.

She is so...*perfect*.

A groan slips from my lips, my cock hardening once more as her hand slips from her center, sliding through the dark triangle of curls and mixing her slick with my spend.

It takes everything within me not to lurch forward and capture her hand, placing her fingers into my mouth. *Everything*.

Her fingers glisten, and I want to taste her.

My spend has covered her, and I expect she will want to clean it off now. My life organ aches at even that thought. But my mate does something I don't expect.

She lifts her hand, bringing it up to her face so she can see her slick mixed in with my spend and then her lids flutter, her eyes falling on me.

I don't know what to expect. I don't want to hope. But when she brings her hand down to the mound on her chest, the tiny bud taut and firm, she rubs my spend there, her eyes never leaving mine as it soaks into her skin.

My cock jerks hard.

"Mona," I groan. But she doesn't stop, and that look in her eyes... In the time since I've known her, I've never seen her look at me like that.

It's captivating. *Addictive.*

I want her to look at me like that for eons. For every waking day of the rest of my existence.

Mona's hand swirls, coated with my spend as she spreads it over her skin and when she adds her other hand, massaging those mounds on her chest till they are shining with my release, I have to plant my knees in the bedding to force myself to keep still.

"Mona..."

Her lids dip slightly. "You said I have to smell like you...right?"

"Yes, but this is..." This is more than I need.

But it's everything I want.

Her eyes watch me like a challenge and I finally move forward, crawling toward her as I lift her leg. Her hands pause in their ministrations and when I set her leg over my thigh, almost so she would straddle me if she rose, a breath shudders from her chest.

Could it be? Could she be as affected as I am?

The back of my neck pulses as my cock jerks between us, brushing against that bunch of curls at her center and smearing more of my spend.

Mona whimpers, I'm sure of it, and the sound takes away some of my control.

I reach forward, my fingers skimming over her waist as I spread my spend across her belly. The sight makes my fangs drip.

And the scent of her. Her arousal...

I don't realize I'm humping her, thrusting my hips forward in a rhythmic sway that pushes my cock against her folds as I continue to massage my release into her skin. But when she bucks against me, pressing my cock back as she grinds her cunt into the base, I'm pulled back to the reality of what we are doing.

She wants this?

She wants...*me*?

Pain, want, and need erupt within me all at once. And I'm reminded for another time just how much of a fool I am.

How could I have denied myself these thoughts? Convinced myself I didn't want this? Believed it for so long?

Because I want this.

No.

I want *her*.

"Mona," I warn, but those eyes of hers are on mine and she doesn't halt. Neither do I. I meet her feverish little thrusts with my own, rubbing the ridges that span my cock into her softness, relishing in the way it makes her eyes roll back and her body shudder.

When a new rush of her arousal, fresher and stronger than ever, reaches my nostrils, all semblance of control is lost.

Her leg is in underneath my hand in a second as I lift it, balancing the roundness of her ass in the other hand just so I can lift her and pull her closer.

Her scent is amazing. Intoxicating. And as a whimper of surprise goes through her, I don't give her the option to pull away.

My tongue dives between her folds, seeking her softness, and as soon as it meets it, I know I am lost.

A rumble goes through my chest as my purr rises and I cannot stop.

This is my mate. No wonder she tastes so qeffing good. I could feast on her like this for days.

Swiping my tongue through her folds, I bury my face into her sweet slit, my nose pressing into her as I breathe in deep.

But I want more.

"Bhihan!" She pants, and I answer. But my words are mumbled against her sweetness. I can't get enough. As she squirms, grinding her soft little cunt into my face, I know I have to pierce her. If even with my tongue. I *need* to.

I do it as slowly as I can, sliding my tongue into her, and Mona screams. It's enough to make me halt, sudden shock and fear going through me.

Did I hurt her?

Did I somehow nick her with my fangs even though I'm trying my hardest to keep them inside my mouth?

"Don't stop," she pants, "Please, don't stop."

Mona's husky words send a shiver through me that makes me push my tongue further, seeking her womb. The place that would hold my kits if I could take this all the way. And as I bob my head, forcing her to ride my tongue, I sense the moment she shatters.

Her whole body quivers as her world comes crashing down around her.

"Bhihan."

Gods, she whimpers my name almost reverently.

I don't deserve this.

"Please," she whimpers.

Reluctantly, I release her, setting her down so our pelvises meet once more, but Mona reaches for me.

"Please," she murmurs, and I can't resist her. So I climb over her till we are face to face, and the look in her eyes is everything I've ever told myself I didn't want. Everything I foolishly told myself I didn't need.

"What do you need, my mate?"

She hesitates for a moment. "You don't have to call me that anymore. Not when we're alone. Not when we're like this. For the first time I..."

"What, my mate?"

She stiffens and that look in her eyes slowly begins to fade.

Panic rises within me.

I've spoilt it. But I want nothing more than for her to look at me like that again.

"I am not pretending." The words tumble from my mouth before I can stop them. And, in the back of my mind, even as the words tumble forth, I wonder if I've always been this horrible at controlling my tongue, or if it's simply the effect of being in her presence. "You are my mate. My *real* mate. The ones the fates have made for me."

She freezes completely, her eyes widening. "What...are you saying?"

I feel I should have kept the truth to myself. That had been the plan anyway. Why the qef am I doing everything opposite to what I decided when it comes to this female?

I have not even marked her yet. She cannot feel the bond and the connection between us is weak.

Where the bond should be is a severed end of something that will probably never take root.

So why can't I follow through? Why does she make me so weak?

I begin to pull away when her hand closes around my bicep, stopping me.

My skin heats at the contact.

"Don't leave."

Her voice is merely above a whisper, enough to send a ripple of desire through me just at the softness of it.

"Tell me what you mean." She gulps, her eyes searching mine. "Is that…" Her chest heaves and I can almost feel her mounting panic. "Is that why you've been doing all this for me? You think I am some mate for you?"

"I don't think you are. I *know* you are."

She will reject me. I can feel it and, already, my life organ aches.

Mona shakes her head. "I…I don't understand. Why do you think this? *How*? When?" Her eyes widen. "Did your shaman tell you something…did they tell you your mate would look like I do? Is that why you risked your life that time, to come after me on that ship? Did you mistake me for—"

I cut her words off as I dip my head and close my lips over hers. Her words die in my mouth and I think she will push me away. Because she resists.

Her lips don't move, but then she whimpers and lets me in.

Need bursts through the center of my being as our tongues collide.

I want this female more than anything. More than my own existence.

When she finally goes, how will I let her be free? How will I survive without her when I am already so helpless from the start?

"You cannot feel it," I whisper against her lips. "Not yet. Not unless I mark you. But I can." I lift my head enough that I can see her face. "You are mine. I am certain of it."

Mona releases a slow breath, watching me the entire time. Her eyes hold suspicion, as if she expects me to betray her at any moment. But there is something else there as well.

Hope.

"How are you so sure? How do you know you're right?"

"Because, Mona, I'll gladly lay down my life for you."

She swallows hard.

"And the only way for me to know what you're saying is true is if you mark me..."

I study her for a moment, caution tightening the muscles in my back.

"Aye."

"So...that's what the king meant when he said I have no mark."

"Aye."

"Why...why don't I have a mark if you're so sure I'm your mate?"

It's clear she doesn't understand what the mark is and I hesitate to answer her. But as with everything else involving this female, my control is weak.

"Because, Mona, the mark is yours to have...but it's one I cannot give you."

23

Mona

I stiffen at his words, my shoulders going rigid as even my hand on his bicep turns to stone. I remove it, pressing my elbows into the straw as I pull myself up and away from him.

What the hell had gotten into me?

It was like I was possessed for a second, forgetting everything about myself and where we were. Who I am. Who *he* is.

I wanted him to fuck me. I wanted him deep inside me, thrusting with abandon. Making me come like he did with his tongue.

Even the memory of it sends a pulse through my clit that I try to ignore.

Because I can't make a mistake. I have to keep my head on my shoulders.

Bhihan eases back, hurt reflecting in his eyes as I move away from him, putting some distance between us, but he doesn't stop me.

Instead, I see resolve in his eyes. As if he's finally admitted something that he'd been holding back for a long time.

He thinks I'm his mate…

I stare at him. The thought won't reconcile in my mind.

I'm not anyone's mate. Females like me don't get married back on New Earth. We stay single forever. And that's alright.

The men on New Earth have always left much to be desired. Countless times, they've let me down. And that's fine all the same, because I decided a long time ago, even before losing my leg and being sent to the Lower Levels, that I didn't want a life partner.

I am better on my own.

But now this...*Atari* is telling me that isn't the case. That I need him.

No. That I am *bonded* to him by forces I don't understand.

I cannot give you my mark.

I turn his words over in my mind, almost afraid to think on them too hard. Because what did he mean by that? Not that I am going to beg him for his mark, whatever that means, but to say he can't give it to me...*why?*

Am I not worthy enough?

"Mona—"

I shake my head and push away the tsunami of emotions surging within me as I reach for the tunic I'd discarded.

I can smell his fresh forest scent in the fibers even though I've been wearing it for a while now, and as I pull it over my head, another scent fills my nostrils. The scent of his cum all over my skin.

It's sweet and intoxicating, like heated caramel, and I remember the thoughts that ran through my mind as I rubbed him into my breasts. I'd wanted to taste it. The only thing that stopped me was the look in his eyes. The absolute need.

I couldn't pull my focus away.

"Mona—" he says again and I shake my head as I shuffle off the bed, my foot hitting the cool floor only seconds later.

Bhihan doesn't say anything as I reach for my crutch and rise.

It's not like I can leave. There's nowhere for me to go anyway. The cell door's locked.

I try not to look at him as I make my way over to the other side of the cell where there's a spout that's made of the same material as the cave bars and the crutch I'm using. It must be water and it activates as soon as I stand before it. There's actually a bowl behind it with some plant-like thing that looks like a loofah.

I take it up as well as the bowl and put both underneath the spout.

The water fills the bowl quickly and I step away, allowing the spout to disengage.

Turning, I can feel his eyes on me as I balance the bowl in one hand and move toward him. Dropping the crutch, I lower myself to the bed and squeeze the thing that looks like a loofah.

It was rock solid when I picked it up. Now it's as soft as cotton.

I squeeze the water from it before turning to Bhihan. Taking my time, I wipe the blood from his chest.

Things moved so fast after he returned from the arena, we didn't even dress his wounds. And I almost begged him to fuck me when he must be filled with aches and sore.

He winces as my fingers touch his skin to steady him, and that's when I finally lift my gaze to his.

What I see there holds me in a daze.

"Why are you…why are you looking at me like that?"

Like a male who is heartbroken and looking at the woman he loves, knowing he must let her go.

I've seen that look in those old movies they still have recorded in the archives.

No one looks at people like that anymore. And yet, he's looking at me as if I mean much more to him than I should.

"Why are you helping me?" Coarse. Rusty. His voice sounds like he hasn't used it for days, even though he just spoke to me minutes before.

My hand stills.

Yes, why am I helping him after everything that's happened? Everything he's said.

Whatever's between us is complicated. And I may not understand it. Heck, I may not understand anything at all, but one thing that I could always rely on was my instincts. What else kept me alive as a kid alone on the streets of Lower Earth? I'd trusted those instincts, kept myself alive until I'd gotten a chance to migrate to the Upper Levels for a better life.

And even though that was short-lived. Even though my accident ripped that sweet life away, it wasn't my instincts that made me fall. It was just dumb luck.

So I'm relying on those senses I can't put a name on as I dip my gaze and continue cleaning his chest.

Despite what's said and happened between us, I can't hold a grudge. And even then, I don't want to.

I just want us to get out of this. Both of us.

And…this male…I want him to be happy.

If anything, he's proven to me that he can be trusted. The male I saw out there fighting, the vicious, cutthroat fighter, is nowhere before me now.

He is a big softie inside…and that's exactly what I need.

Whatever demons he's hiding… Whatever things he doesn't want to let me know… That's okay.

No one has ever stuck their neck out for me the way he's doing now, and that's all I need to keep in mind. Everything else doesn't matter.

"Isn't this what mates do?" I huff a small laugh through my nose and force a smile on my lips.

I don't believe what he says one bit. Maybe the Darzel's toxin did more than made him paralyzed on that ship and it's interrupting his natural instincts. Whatever it is, it too will clear up.

A shiver goes through him as I reach up over his shoulder to brush the alien loofah across his ears. They twitch and I smile before dipping the thing into the bowl and squeezing the water from it again.

Silence descends between us, the only sound being Bhihan's unsteady breaths every time my fingers brush against his skin.

I work slowly, enjoying the intimacy of it all.

This is the first time since this began that I have had a moment to breathe. And I don't want it to end.

When I finish, I set the bowl down on the floor, ready to grasp my crutch so I can take it back to the water spout, but I'm suddenly pulled backward, my world spinning as Bhihan's arms encircle me. He spins with me, turning us together on the straw until he's holding me like I'm the little spoon.

There's a moment where my heart lurches, uncertainty of old coming to the fore, but as Bhihan dips his head to my shoulder, burying his face into my neck as he inhales deeply, all of that uncertainty seeps away.

We don't say a word. Neither of us speaks. He simply holds me.

There's no wall between us.

And for the first time in my life, I feel…free.

24

Bhihan

She's so soft. Feeling her here against me, the way she melds to me like an extension of my being, I know I am inching closer and closer to never being able to let her go.

So I hold her tight, even as the light from the star leaves this room and I know we have spent a whole cycle on this planet. I hold her. My mate.

My fangs have been aching since I tasted her slick.

Big mistake.

Now I can't get the taste of her off my tongue, and what's worse, I dread the moment her taste fades.

Her body rises and falls as she sleeps, and I groan as I inhale her skin.

She smells like me. Like my spend has soaked into her pores. And it only makes me want her more. To lift her leg and slide my throbbing cock between her folds. To fill her up with my release till she is bursting from within.

I want it so badly, an ache goes through my fangs as I bury my nose harder against her skin.

It would be so easy to do it. If I mark her, sink my fangs into her soft skin and deposit my life spirit, securing the bond between us, then this ache, this pain, it would all stop.

But I can't.

She moves against me one more time and I hiss, pain shooting through my cock *and* my fangs.

This isn't good.

I know the need to rut consumes most males when they find their mates, but it has only been a short time since I discovered Mona is mine. This pain…this *ache*…I know what it means, even if I don't want to face it.

For those males who ignore the bond, it can drive them insane. And if I am going insane, that only means I need to get Mona out of here before I lose my mind.

When she moves again and I groan, pain shooting through my fangs so much that I almost bare them against her skin, she whimpers my name.

"Bhihan?"

I freeze.

I don't want her to witness me like this. Weak. Yearning for her. But most of all, desperately trying to regain control.

"Are you okay? You sound like you're in pain." I let her continue speaking, loving the sound of her husky voice. I want to hear her scream my name with that voice as I stretch her tight little hole. I want to hear her whimper and beg me to rut her and make her release on my cock, my tongue, my fingers…

Each thought sends an image into my mind and I groan again.

This time she stiffens and attempts to look back at me, but I hold her still.

"I can…check those wounds for you again. They looked small, but maybe they're like paper cuts. Small, but hurt like hell."

"No," I groan. "This is not a result of my wounds."

She tries to move again, but I won't let her. Each time she shifts, her supple little behind rubs against my cock in the most tempting of ways.

Does she have any idea what I want to do to her?

"And your skin…" I can hear the alarm rising on her tongue. "Y-you're burning up, Bhihan."

"Normal."

"Normal?! You weren't burning up like this earlier. I don't think this is normal."

"It's because of you."

She stiffens again, and I know I should guard my words, maybe explain a little. But the more she speaks, the more her voice strokes against me and the more I notice the softness that she is melded to me. I can't think straight.

"Me?"

I can almost sense her thinking. I want to know her thoughts.

That pit inside me where the bond lies untethered lights up as the bond reaches toward her, seeking completion.

I want to feel her highs. I want to be there for her lows. I want to know her thoughts and what pushes her to be all I never thought she was.

I want to know everything about her.

I hold her tighter and she winces.

"Bhihan, you're starting to make me worry."

"At the end of this, my mate, you must forgive me."

She shakes her head. "Forgive you why? You've been nothing but good to me, even though you think I'm something I'm not, but…" She releases a breath and relaxes against me. "I guess, when you come back to your senses, you'll regret all of this, too. So…it is I who must ask for your forgiveness."

"What did you say?" An ache goes through me.

"Sorry for everything. For getting you involved in this fight that isn't yours. And…I'm sorry you think I'm your mate. I understand now that's why you're putting yourself in such danger for me. It's not…it's not right. And I'm sorry."

It is my turn to stiffen and I spin her in my arms so she can face me.

I may not be the male she needs, but I won't let her live thinking that I have done all this because of some mistake.

"There is no mistake that you are mine."

She scoffs and drops her gaze from mine.

"You don't feel it, but I do." I move my hand to where that pit is in my chest. Where the bond sways untethered. "Here."

"I'm not a fool, Bhihan," she says after a few moments, her whisper carrying across my skin like a soft but sad caress. "If I was really your mate, you would have marked me."

Her throat moves as she swallows hard before releasing a breath. "I know why and I'm not like…angry with you or anything." She huffs a mirthless laugh through her nose. "Things like that don't hurt anymore."

Despite the ache going through me, I tilt her chin so she is meeting my eyes. Her eyes have a sheen that only highlights the sadness filling her pupils.

I put that there. That sadness.

She is hurting right now because of me.

I must fix it. Despite my oath to keep my maw shut and get through this without revealing much, I *have* to tell her.

I cannot bear seeing her like this.

"Whatever you believe, Mona, you are wrong."

She simply looks at me before her gaze drops and I have to force her to look at me again.

"I cannot mark you. And I *want* to…I want to more than anything. But I'll risk insanity and pain that comes with not fulfilling this bond if it will mean I can save one female in this cursed bloodline of mine."

She blinks at me. "What…do you mean?"

Alarm bells ring through my head, but now that I have started talking, I can't stop.

"My mark is…venomous."

She blinks at me again, confusion furrowing her brow. "What?"

"If I mark you, my life spirit will make you insane." A shudder goes through me, more from painful memories than anything else. "It happened to the female that birthed me."

"Your mother."

"I do not refer to her as such. She hated me and everything I represented. I was only a kit, but I remember her screaming and tearing at her skin, trying to rip the threads of my father's life spirit from her veins."

Mona swallows hard again, eyes widening slightly. "How…how do you mark your mate?"

"With these." I bare my fangs before her, a shiver going through me. I can't hold back as some life spirit squirts from the tip of my fangs and into my mouth. They are bursting with the need to release into my mate.

No wonder I am burning up.

"Your fangs are like a snake's? Is that venom that just squirted from them?"

I stare at her.

I did not expect her to have this reaction. If I had told an Atari female what I just told Mona, she would be moving far away from me. Males like me are cursed.

But Mona is not Atari.

If anything, what I have just disclosed seems to have made her more…*interested*.

"A sneks?"

She smiles. "It was a creature that lived on Old Earth. They don't exist anymore. But they had fangs like you do and some had venom." Her eyes widen slightly. "Oh…you'd bite me with those? Put venom inside me…but…that doesn't make sense. Why would your bite be venomous?"

She searches my eyes, waiting for an answer.

She doesn't pull away. She doesn't look disgusted. She doesn't appear to be alarmed.

"It…is not supposed to be."

She still looks at me the same way. There is nothing in her eyes to make me believe she would rather be anywhere else than beside me right now. And it…throws me off guard.

"Mona…"

"Then *why* is it venomous?"

"I wish I could answer you, my mate. When I first realized this curse was present in my bloodline, I searched high and low for a reason. I found none."

She watches me with interest.

"My father's brother did the same to his mate. She took her own life. And his son did the same. His mate itched to get rid of him so badly that she succeeded where my mor could not in ripping her skin to shreds. She lives sedated on Atar. A living corpse."

A breath shudders from me, a weight I didn't know I'd been carrying finally leaving my shoulders.

I told her. I told her the truth. The weight of a truth I've been carrying for so long.

And...she hasn't run away.

"So...I'm your mate...and you can't claim the bond so I can feel it...because you think doing so will cause me to go insane..." Her lips come together as she blinks at me. And then...she laughs.

Mona throws her head back and her body shudders with mirth.

I stare at her, confused. The sound of her laughter fills me with happiness. I want to hear her laugh all the time, every day. I want her joy. I crave it.

But, her laughter only means one thing. She is relieved. Or she does not understand the severity of this.

"Bhihan," she sobers, wiping a tear from her eye, "I'm already insane."

"Mona."

"I'm not laughing at your concerns. If anything, it warms my heart so much that you've gone through all this pain of holding that information back because you were thinking of *me*." She lifts a hand to my jaw. "No one has ever cared about me that much to go through such an extent to keep me safe, even from themselves. Bhihan..." She's completely sober now and her words make a tightness develop all throughout my being. I'm almost afraid to hear what else she has to say. Almost afraid to hear the rejection that I've been running from all this time. "I understand now. I understand it all. But...this is doing something to you, isn't it..."

Her fingers skirt over my skin and I lean into her touch.

She is not afraid of me? Disgusted by me?

This is not what I imagined.

"You have a fever and every time I move, you wince. You're in pain, aren't you."

My throat moves and that seems to be enough answer for her.

"You need to bite me now that your instincts have kicked in…"

Again, I don't answer her. The more she speaks, the more I get the sense that she is going to request something that I'll never do. I draw the line at sinking my fangs into her neck.

I refuse.

"What happens if you don't bite me?" she whispers.

"I'll live."

She studies me, eyes too intelligent. "Will you though?"

I break from her gaze, unable to lie to her face. We do not yet share a bond and she can already read me so easily.

Qef me.

"You don't need to worry about me."

"Fuck that."

When I glance at her, she is frowning up at me like a little dachsheen with tiny teeth.

I almost laugh.

My mate is adorable.

But any warm feelings that were about to spring from me are shut down the moment I sense a change in the air.

The back of my neck pulses and my eyes shoot outside the cell bars. I wish to spend days like this in Mona's arms, basking in her acceptance. But our time together has ended.

As sound comes through the corridor and I see the first Darzel, it becomes clear we are no longer alone.

25

Mona

"The scent of your mating is strong in this space."

The sound of the Darzel king makes me startle as Bhihan growls toward one of the tunnels.

The king appears shortly after, walking slowly, as if he has all the time in the world. And just like that, whatever safe space I'd cocooned myself in with Bhihan these last few hours disappears.

His eyes are on me. Unreadable. Yet, I get the sense he was hoping for some other occurrence. Some other result. Maybe for me to not have a scent on me at all, just so he could watch me die before his eyes.

Scum.

"Rise, Atari." The king's eyes slide from me to Bhihan, and I feel a low growl go through him. "Your next conquest awaits."

Wait, what?

So soon?

"He's in no condition to fight again. Not yet." I frown, rising into a sitting position.

"That is no concern to me…female." For the first time since being in the presence of this alien, I hear a tinge of annoyance in his tone. For sure, he's pissed that we "mated". Thank God Bhihan's idea worked… even though I probably would have not been afraid to do the real thing.

A blush spreads across my cheeks as he rises, semi-hard cock swinging.

The Darzel pay no attention to it, as if they're used to this level of nakedness. I suppose, for those jewels they wear seem to be the only form of clothing they put on. But for me, this is not usual.

I can't help but stare at Bhihan as he slips back into his trou, his muscles flexing and bunching as he moves.

He is perfection.

And he is mine?

Yes. Mine.

The thought makes me swallow hard.

"I'm ready," he says, and my wild thoughts disappear as I'm suddenly thrown back into reality.

He's about to go out there again to fight? But we haven't solved the problem of this mate thing yet. His body is protesting. His fever is rising. Surely, those aren't the best conditions to run into an arena with.

"Good," the king coos. "Your opponent today will be a special one."

My chest tightens at those words and I reach for Bhihan, grabbing his hand. He turns to look at me, warmth in his eyes before he offers me a smile. But it does nothing to reassure me.

We have to get out of this place.

We have to get free because I can't…I can't lose him.

The thought hits me like a brick and far too late. Something clenches inside me as Bhihan's fingers slip from mine and he exits the cell.

As last time, two Darzel wait for me to exit too and I hurry to pull on my boot before following them out to the small underground room.

When I get there, the crowd is already going wild in the stands.

It seems that Bhihan's previous performance has only made them thirst for more, and as I grip the bars, scanning the grounds for sight of him, I can't help the tension that crawls up my spine.

This isn't sustainable. Each time he goes out there, the chances of him not returning multiply. And today, I don't trust what the king has in store.

The last battle was quick and I hope this one will be too, but something curdles in my gut as I squint against the bright sun seeping into this underground room.

Something's making me scared far beyond the situation that's presented before us.

Something deep down is making me terrified.

And I don't know what it is.

The king appears on his throne above the tunnel the monsters come through and the crowd hushes. As before he waves his hand and my gaze snaps to the side where I see Bhihan enter the arena.

The crowd erupts again and my hands tighten even more on the bars.

I'm scared.

Why am I so scared?

I've seen him fight. He's incredible. And I know he can take care of himself.

So why does my stomach feel so sour? Like it's filled with the poison of dread?

I don't even realize the two Darzel who are supposed to be watching me leave me alone like before. All I can focus on is Bhihan as he enters the arena and turns to face me.

My heart lurches.

No. It *aches*, creating a pull toward him that wasn't there before.

I want to go out there and help him. I *should* be out there helping him. But I know more than anything that I'd be a hindrance.

I can't help him.

Instead, I have to stay here, waiting. Hoping.

His back is turned to the king, an obvious disrespect, but he doesn't seem to care. And I watch as he raises his hand, closing his fist as he hits it against his chest.

No. His *heart*.

He's saluting me.

Something inside me thumps hard as tears rise in my eyes and when the king raises his hand again, the crowd gets even louder. But even the deafening noise of the Darzel cannot dampen the sound that comes from the tunnel.

It's a sound I've never heard before and one that makes my breath cease in my throat.

Still focused on me, Bhihan doesn't even turn to look and I want to scream.

Did he not hear that?

It sounds like a lion. Deep bellows and roars that end with a hiss.

I grip the bars tighter, pressing my face against them as I step on tiptoe, heart hammering in my chest as I try to see.

The crowd cheers, almost growing manic with anticipation, and even as they scream and shout their praises, Bhihan stands still, looking at me.

That sound in the tunnel gets louder, enough to vibrate the air, and it's clear that whatever it is, it's big. Fucking big. And dangerous, judging from the Darzel's reaction.

The earth shakes, and it's not like the day before with that wild cat thing. It's different this time. Like a rumble that spreads from the tunnel outward, vibrating through the dry ground.

Small particles of dirt pebble before the cage bars like tiny balls bouncing. The movement starts slow. One thump and the little balls move. Then two. Three. Until they're vibrating, no pause between them, and when I lift my gaze, my breath stops in my throat.

Something huge comes through the tunnel and I almost stagger back as if it was right before me.

Dark brown fur covers every inch of the huge beast that charges into the arena, a cloud of dust in its wake.

The warthog. It's the frickin warthog, and it's even bigger and more terrifying than on that holo vid. It's clear now that the alien I'd seen it chasing had been three times my size, because the beast looks like it should have existed millennia ago, when gigantic creatures like the dinosaurs roamed Old Earth.

The thing roars and for a moment, Bhihan disappears from view, enveloped by the dust.

The creature is so large, its head rises above the cloud, sharp ivory tusks pointed to the air as it roars again. The earth shakes as it stomps and turns in a slow circle and the Darzel go crazy.

This is their champion. Their star. And mine is…

My heart thumps hard as I search the dust cloud for a sign of Bhihan.

For a moment, that fear inside my chest heightens and I worry he might have been trampled by the beast. It's still stomping and moving in a circle until it suddenly stops and snorts.

All of a sudden, it doesn't look like the angry raging beast it first appeared as.

It snorts again as it eyes the crowd, and this time when it turns, it's with measured calculation, as if it is…looking for something.

The dust clears slowly, and the crowd dies down to a hush. It's quiet enough that the creature's low snorts reach my ear. Like hot air going inside a deep hole only to hiss back out like a small geyser, the creature moves slowly and sniffs.

And then I see him. His outline as the dust clears. Bhihan.

The crowd erupts.

There he is, standing in the same spot, but this time, he's turned away from me. His eyes are on the creature and my heart aches.

He looks so small in front of it as it stands like a tower before him.

And then he moves, so fast he is but a blur.

For a moment, it seems the creature is as surprised as everyone else to see him standing there, and when he darts toward it, it doesn't react fast enough.

But then it roars, head dipping almost to the ground like a bull ready to charge. Those white tusks look ready to cut the approaching Atari, and the beast bellows before meeting his charge. It dashes forward, dust kicking up all around, and Bhihan jumps.

I have no idea how he launches himself so high in the air when he's made of so much muscle. He's heavy, but he looks as light as a feather as he goes airborne. The monster misses and tries to halt its charge, but the momentum carries it forward and it has a hard time stopping itself.

It skids, huge hooves digging grooves into the dry earth as it carries on moving forward until it's so close to my side of the arena that I can smell its stench.

The crowd shouts and for a moment, I'm just staring into the eyes of the beast.

It lifts its colossal head and shakes it, eyes looking a bit dazed.

How the hell do you kill something like this? There's just no way. You'd need a sword like three times my size to pierce this thing and cause damage.

It's as big as a dragon. We're probably lucky it doesn't breathe fire.

As soon as that thought leaves my mind, the beast spits. It's a bubbling pile of green that fizzes as it hits the dirt and seeps down into the dry earth.

Acid?

Well, shit.

As the beast turns and readies itself to charge again, it scrapes its back legs into the earth, causing dust to billow my way. I almost don't see as Bhihan does the same thing, disorienting the creature and making it charge right into the arena wall.

Several unlucky Darzel fall from the stands as a result of the sudden shockwave, arms flailing as they meet the ground below.

The creature snorts and I can't look away as it rips them all apart.

Their goo doesn't even protect them. The monster's dark fur acts as a barrier as it tramples and pierces them with its tusks.

I expect the Darzel standing over the carnage to scream and disperse.

Instead, more come forward to take the seats of their fallen people, screaming and frothing at the lips with complete glee.

How…how can they be so…utterly unrepentant?

Goo and the blood of its enemies hanging from its tusks, the monster turns in Bhihan's direction, and without hesitation, it charges once more.

This time, Bhihan turns away from the monster and runs.

The Darzel pause like a collective before they erupt.

To them, it looks like he is running away from the beast after seeing what it just did to their people, but I've seen this male face the nothingness of the void to save a female he didn't even know.

I know him better.

The only time I've seen fear in his eyes is when he's been looking at me. Fear *for* me. And I know without a doubt that he's not running from that monster because he is scared.

He's running because he has a plan.

My fingers tighten on the bars till I feel pain in my palms, the seconds moving slowly as Bhihan races to the opposite end of the arena. The beast is right behind him, head lowering as it charges, tusks pointed forward, ready to impale its target and sure of it. But, at the last moment, just before it catches up to him, Bhihan veers.

The creature can't stop. It's too late and it crashes into the arena wall. Several large blocks fall with the impact, breaking as they hit the ground along with over a dozen Darzel who lose their balance.

There's a cloud of dust, but I can almost see the stars circling the creature's head. It's confused, in a daze after hitting its head that hard, and I finally realize what Bhihan is doing.

In the chaos of the Darzel shouting and trying to climb back up into the stands—while several of their counterparts thwart their efforts by pushing them back in—Bhihan grabs one of the huge blocks that fell in the monster's destruction.

He jumps, launching himself high enough to take a foothold on one of the animal's tusks before he jumps again onto the creature's nose.

With his first utterance, a roar that sounds like a great war cry, Bhihan slams the block into the creature's eye.

It bellows, throwing its head back so hard that Bhihan loses his foothold. He falls and I almost climb through the bars.

It's going to trample him! It's going to—

As the creature kicks up dirt, spinning and roaring, shaking its head in pain, I see several Darzel get squished to death. But I can't see Bhihan.

I'm almost overcome with anxiety when I see a flash of bronze skin and there, climbing the broken wall of the stands, Bhihan climbs upward till he is high above the creature.

The moment the monster sees him is the same moment the Darzel in the stands do. Their screams erupt even louder as Bhihan throws himself from the wall, rock in hand.

His aim is clear as he descends, the force carrying him and putting power into the blow he lands in the monster's other eye.

It roars, head shaking and my heart thumps.

My man is smart. So smart. He blinded it.

My heart thumps hard.

My man?

Mine?

As the beast bellows, shaking its head in distress, a few more Darzel still on the ground get trampled as Bhihan walks to the center of the arena.

The beast can't see him anymore but it snorts as if trying to smell him and find the source of his next attack.

But there is none.

And as Bhihan faces the Darzel king, I realize what he wants.

A weapon.

Unlike before, they did not throw down a sword. What did they think he was going to use to kill this thing?

Thin air?

Fuck!

Anger rises within me.

If he didn't use his ingenuity, he wouldn't have been able to wound the thing.

The Darzel king lifts his hand almost reluctantly and the crowd cheers. A weapon that looks like a huge spear lands in the dirt not far from Bhihan and I see the moment he reaches for it.

With all of the Darzel on the ground now dead, the beast twists and turns, snorting as it pulls great amounts of air into its nostrils. And then it turns, as if it can smell Bhihan, it turns and roars in his direction.

When it charges, I don't expect it to be so accurate with its eyes no longer of use, but it is. It heads directly toward him and Bhihan crouches, pressing one end of the spear in the dirt as he braces.

He doesn't move as the thing races toward him and the Darzel erupt in screams of anticipation.

Either he will take the monster down, or he will die.

As the creature comes upon him, its lack of vision makes it miss its mark. It knows which direction he's in, but not exactly where. And Bhihan uses that to his advantage.

As the beast reaches striking point, Bhihan surges the spear forward, piercing the creature's side.

There's a pained cry, one so loud it echoes in the arena, and the Darzel hush. But as the beast staggers and falls, they erupt again.

A breath shudders from me. He's done it.

He's really done it.

I can't believe it.

But that coil of fear is still in my belly and I try to push it away as I grin and watch Bhihan. He'll return to me now. All will be fine.

But he doesn't turn to leave the stadium.

Instead, I watch as he falls to his knees, his body going almost boneless before he collapses into the dirt.

Time stops.

"Bhihan!"

26

Bhihan

They've tricked me.

The moment I stepped into this arena, I knew the Darzel king was up to something.

Even while fighting the mokrass, I wondered what his angle would be. I know now.

As I fall to my knees and the Darzel cheer, the only thing on my mind is the female that's locked in the cells behind me.

I cannot fail her.

But despite the need to remain standing, to keep fighting, my body fails me.

It's the Darzel king.

This weapon he sent me.

My eyes slide to it as I fall.

It's imbued with his essence, made with the same goo that falls from his body in sheets.

I can see it now, small crystals embedded in the strange material the Darzel use for almost everything on this world.

Qeffing nuisance.

He has no honor.

My limbs become useless as my life organ slows down. I am vulnerable, and my female is even more so now that I am down. But no matter how I try to fight the effect of the toxin, it's of no use.

I am sure he intends for me to be out of commission for a few yora, maybe even days. But what he doesn't know is that I've been exposed to Darzel toxin before. Even before I encountered Mona.

And each time, recovery is shortened.

I'll be on my feet in the next few minutes. They don't know that, but I do and till then, I have to hope I wounded that beast enough that it doesn't come to find me.

But even as I send this hope to the gods of Atar, the beast staggers, trying to rise. Its wound. It isn't fatal.

It will come to finish the job with the Darzel king on its side.

And I should have known.

Mokrass are rare titans of an age long gone. To have one in his possession, the Darzel king must have traded much. To lose such a beast will create friction with his people when he can no longer entertain them with the viciousness of the mokrass.

The ground shudders beneath me as the mokrass tries to rise again but fails. I pierced its life organ. I am sure of my aim. But the wound must not have been deep enough.

Qef.

As it tries again and fails, the Darzel shout in anticipation. They aren't sure if it will manage the feat, but I am positive it will.

The beast is enraged. Thirsty for my blood.

There is no way for me to survive this if the toxin doesn't leave my system soon. And I have to.

For my Mona.

I can even hear her voice, screaming my name. Even through the noise the Darzel make, I can hear her still.

My Mona.

My sweet, fierce, Mona.

"Bhihan!"

I hear her shout through the roars of the Darzel in the stands, far too close to my ears. As if she is in the arena with me. And when a shadow is cast above me, my whole world stands still.

Mona?

I cannot say her name but I want to scream it.

Mona!

She is here. By my side, terror in her eyes as she falls to her knee, dropping her walking aid to grasp my shoulder.

"Bhihan, what happened to you? Where are you hurt? Where's the wound?"

I can't believe she is here. What is she doing here? It's not safe.

Not far from us, the mokrass thunders, still trying to rise, and the earth shakes.

Mona must leave here now.

I grunt, unable to form words as she braces against me and rolls me to my back. Then all I can see is her beautiful face as it blocks out the star. Her tear-filled eyes.

Her fingers tremble as her hands hover over my frame. She's searching for a wound but there is none. Nothing critical. I have not been pierced by the beast and I wish I could use my tongue. To tell her that she needs to return to the safety of the cell.

How did she even get out here? Why did the Darzel let her escape?

But I already know the answer to that.

They have almost gone silent as they watch us now.

This is entertainment for them, and this is an episode they have never witnessed before. Two beings together, completely focused on one another when death is so near, and my heart aches at the thought that Mona abandoned safety so she could come save me.

Even with the mokrass in the background thundering and shaking the earth in its efforts to rise, she does not seem to notice the danger.

Her complete focus is on me and making sure that *I* am safe.

My dear Mona…

She might not feel the bond, but it's there. In her own human way…she…*cares* for me.

"It's the toxin, isn't it?" she says, eyes going hard as the tears within them seep away. She turns her gaze in the direction of the king and I swear my female snarls.

Vicious this female. I think I love her.

Gods, who am I trying to fool?

I am besotted by her.

She is already my everything.

I would take on this whole world just to save her.

And that is why I need to move.

Fighting my own being, I try to move. I try to push past the toxin's effects and save my female. Because if she is ripped apart here, before my eyes, I'll never forgive myself, and every Darzel in this arena will pay for it.

But no matter how I fight, I cannot move. All that occurs is a twitching in my fingers.

It is happening. The toxin's effect is lessening. But it's not happening quickly enough. And right now, seconds are like minutes. Every click counts.

"That's it."

At first, I don't realize Mona had spoken until she rises.

There is murmuring in the crowd of Darzel that quickly rises to a loud hum. They are confused.

I am confused.

Mona, I try to call her but nothing comes from my mouth.

What is she doing?

Stretching toward the star, Mona grips my tunic that she wears and pulls it up over her head.

Now she is almost bare before the seedy eyes of the Darzel, only her strange undergarments hiding a bit of her sweet skin, and a surge of protectiveness goes through me.

She is the most beautiful thing I have ever seen. Sculpted by the great Gods of Atar themselves. Even just looking at her now, I am in awe.

The star's light plays against her skin, warming it and making it glow and I know that if we survive this, I must take her back to Atar where the starlight will bless her every day. Because my female is meant to be celebrated. And I'll celebrate her. Even if she cannot bear my mark, I'll celebrate her for as long as she will allow me to.

My thoughts clear somewhat when Mona wraps the tunic around

her hands, almost like she's restraining herself. But when she reaches for the spear, I realize all she's done is completely cover her hands.

What is she…

Wait. She reached for the spear. She couldn't be thinking—

But as Mona turns away from me and braces on the spear, using it as her walking aid as she heads toward the thrashing mokrass, my life organ lurches in my chest.

No.

I struggle to rise, only managing to lift my body partially, but not enough to be mobile. As my back thumps against the dirt once more, an ache I never knew develops in my chest.

Mona. No. She can't.

Despite my efforts, only a grunt escapes me and she pauses to look over her shoulder.

Those hardened eyes lock with mine and I'm reminded of the female I caught hanging on the side of a freaking ship in the void. That stubborn, rude little female. *My* stubborn, rude little female. And I know whatever's in her head, her mind's made up.

She's a survivor. And she wants us to make it. Not just herself. But…me too.

But I can't let her. I can't let her face that thing alone.

So I force myself to move, my body not cooperating. Failing me. Failing *her*.

Mona smiles as she looks at me. It's a sad smile, one that doesn't reach her eyes.

One that's like a goodbye.

But I'm not ready to say goodbye. Qef it. I don't want to say goodbye at all.

Staring up into the skies, I curse the gods. I curse the fates. And I curse this body of mine.

"It'll be okay." Mona's voice cuts through the loud murmurs of the Darzel and into my consciousness, and as I watch her turn and approach the mokrass, my world goes dim.

About three lengths away from the huge animal, Mona halts, leaning on the spear as she tilts her head back to lock eyes with the

Darzel king. Whatever passes between them makes her snarl enough that I see her teeth.

Her chest heaves as she braces on the spear pointing it forward. And my female…she roars.

If I wasn't terrified out of my skin, I would have marveled at the war sound that comes from my female's lips. But all I can hear is that I am failing her.

At the sound she makes, the mokrass and the Darzel react. While the Darzel cheer, the beast snorts, no doubt picking up her scent. With thunderous beats of its hind legs against the earth, it struggles to rise, and seeing its effort, I do the same.

I cannot let it rise first.

Compared to the beast, Mona looks like a kit standing before it. But she does not falter. Even when time stops still and the beast staggers to its feet.

The noise from the Darzel is deafening. They ache to see her end. And Mona…Mona remains completely focused. She does not see them. She does not see me.

All she sees is the monster that has risen before her and as she remains still, I wonder if she is frozen in fear.

Run.

"Run!" The word croaks from my lips as I flip from my back to my belly. Can I crawl? If I have to do so I'll and I try, forcing my arms to pull me across the dirt.

But even as I move, even as I reach for the hope the fates dangle before me, the mokrass charges.

And Mona stands in place.

27

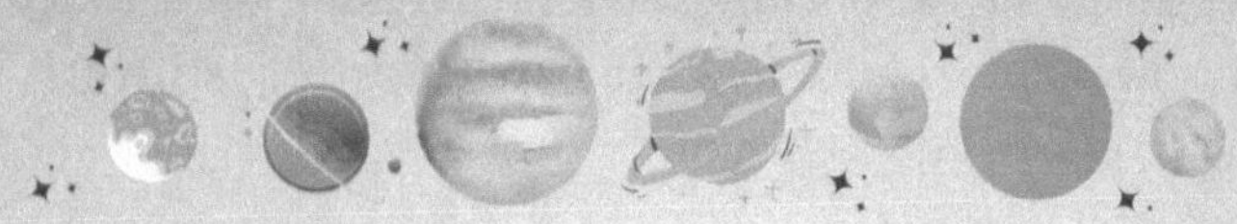

Everything within my being shatters to pieces the moment the mokrass charges. Mona crouches, putting all her weight into the butt of the spear as the sharp point pierces the air. And though her hands are almost bound, she clings on to the weapon.

And then I understand. I understand why she stripped the tunic. Why she's covered her hands.

The Darzel venom can't pierce her skin through the tunic, but that's the least of my worries now.

"Mona!" I can't move as the mokrass collides with her. There is no other way to describe it.

One moment she is there, and the next, she has disappeared from view. Unlike any sane person, she stood unmoving, leaning all her weight into the weapon. Trusting in the one thing I told her about this material the Darzel use. By remaining still, if she hit her target, all the power the mokrass exerted would be transferred right back to it.

It's smart.

But it's also insane.

Dust clouds the surface as the mokrass roars and my world stops.

I can't see her.

No.

"Mona!"

The noise that erupts in the arena swallowed my roar; the Darzel rejoicing at the victory of their champion while I can hardly breathe.

My world.

It's shattering. Red clouding my vision even as I stare, hoping that reality is wrong.

But the mokrass roars again, its huge head flailing backward in slow motion and even the lifeblood in my veins ceases to move. For that is not a normal movement.

And as the huge beast tilts, its body smashing into the earth and another dust cloud envelops the arena, the Darzel hush.

In the silence, no sound comes from the beast.

It is…dead.

Mona…killed it?

The hush in the arena is proof of her feat. The Darzel are, for the first time since I've heard of their games, speechless.

Well, qef them.

A grunt goes through me as I crawl across the ground and soon my legs come back online and I am staggering toward the mokrass' corpse.

My female. My Mona.

My life organ has shattered to pieces in my chest.

I don't know what I'll find when I get there, but I dread what I'll see.

But as I stagger forward, in the silence of the arena, I hear a hiss and a grunt. I almost stumble with the sudden surge of hope that fills me.

Mona?

The mokrass' huge body is in the way and I have to force my limbs to assist me as I climb over one of its huge legs. There, on the other side, covered in bruises and dirt, is Mona.

Brown eyes that have seen too much pain turn my way and I collapse before her, chest heaving with the urge to breathe, reminding me I've been holding my breath all this time.

"Mona," I breathe as I pull her into my arms.

She coughs, trying to expel the dust that has gotten into her lungs, and I have never been more grateful in my life.

"You stubborn female." I grip her tighter. "You stubborn, stubborn female."

She coughs again and leans into me, hands clasping my neck as she uses me for strength and I let her melt against me.

Nothing has ever felt this good than to have her in my arms.

"Never," cough, "Never ever doing that again. I almost pissed myself when it charged."

I want to grip her and berate her for putting herself in such danger, but how can I take her victory away from her? I see the spear now, sticking out of the mokrass's side, right in the wound I'd inflicted first.

"You're so qeffing smart," I mutter instead, holding her so close, she's almost a part of me. "But if you do anything like that again, I'll have to lock you in my quarters and punish you."

She coughs, but I hear a giggle, too. "That's not a threat, big guy."

Her slight giggle is what makes my ears twitch. What causes me to finally take my attention from her to notice the utter silence around us. And when I look up, the Darzel king's beady eyes are settled on us.

Unease writhes across my being, the nape of my neck pulsing with alarm.

He rises slowly, watching us, and the crowd of Darzel grows quieter still.

I can almost feel the anger emanating from his being and his intentions become even clearer.

He never intended for us to win; he certainly never intended to let it get this far.

Their champion lies motionless, while we are still breathing.

Gripping Mona, I pull her into my arms as I rise to stand.

I am done playing his games. Our sacrifice here has already been too great and what I almost lost…nothing could have ever sufficed for that.

So I hold my mate close. I feel her warmth. And I know that we are leaving this place. Somehow.

Whatever debt I owed these beings has been repaid.

But I head towards the exit, my neck pulses hard, and all I feel is the slight brush of air as something shoots past me, hitting Mona in the center of her chest.

She hisses, inhaling sharply as her eyes widen, and when my gaze falls on the object, reality cracks around me.

I've never seen it before, so I don't know how I know exactly what it is as soon as my eyes land on it.

Thin as a needle with a small fluid sack at the end, I stare at the weapon that has pierced my mate.

"Bhihan, what's—"

Her eyes suddenly roll back, her body convulsing.

The toxin.

I grip the needle, pulling it from her skin, rage filling me as I turn my eyes on the Darzel king.

He did this.

A roar thunders from me as I fall to my knees, eyes on Mona.

I've seen no Atari react to Darzel toxin like this. But then again, I have never seen the toxin's effect on a female, only seasoned warriors in training. And it was never injected, only topically applied.

But this fiend…

Mona's body seizes and shakes, her lids fluttering as she grasps for me, but even when she has my arm she still claws for my skin. As if she's drowning and screaming for me to help her.

"What have you done?!" My roar echoes in the arena at the same time that I hear the Darzel king's command.

"Seize him!"

Several Darzel race from the stands and I know I have a split second to decide what to do.

Spinning, I catch sight of the spear still jutting from the mokrass' side and it pains me as I slip my arms from my mate's and set her on the ground.

"Mona. Forgive me."

Unwrapping the tunic from her wrists, my fingers are feverish as I race back toward the beast. Gripping the spear, I pull it from the creature's flesh and turn.

Another roar goes through me as I launch it.

I know he doesn't expect it. Confident he doesn't see it coming.

And when the spear pierces the king's head, sending him flying backward on his throne, the pleasure that one action should give me is nowhere to be found.

All I feel is terror.

They've taken her away from me *again*.

Qef diplomacy. I killed their king. No way he'll survive his skull being split open. And that means the Darzel will now be at war with Atar. I wish I could care.

I only have a few minutes to do this. To get us out of here.

The moment the king dies is the moment the Darzel go haywire. War breaks out in the stands, each vying for a spot on the throne.

It is enough distraction for me to race across the mokrass' frame, eyes searching with frantic desperation for my mate's walking stick.

I almost miss it, if not a Darzel who comes flying through the air and landing right near it.

I grip it, racing back to the mokrass where I open its giant maw and cover the stick with its acid.

This will do.

It will *have* to do.

Every moment away from Mona is breaking me apart, and when I finally reach her side and she grips on to me, my heart breaks again.

The look in her eyes, as if she'd thought I'd left her here, makes a cavern open up inside me. And I know, at this moment I know, I'll be lost without her.

Hoisting her into my arms, I run across the arena.

Chaos still ensuing everywhere, none of the Darzel seem to notice us and when I reach the gate that leads through the tunnels and spot one in my way, I know he's the unlucky qeffer I'll use.

"You," I growl and the Darzel turns, beady eyes widening as he shivers. His eyes drop to the acid bubbling on the walking aid and he takes a few steps backward, seemingly more terrified of what I have in my hand than he is terrified of me.

"Lead me to a craft. *Now!*"

"I—I canno—"

"You are just one of many I can find to do this. Choose, or die." I am past bargaining and he must see it in my eyes because he turns, opening the gate and hurrying through the tunnels. I follow him, gripping Mona to me as she continues to shake.

Her body is trying to reject the invasion, but it can't. She needs the cure.

"Where is the cure for your toxin?"

The Darzel hurrying before me glances over his shoulder, his gaze falling on Mona, and at my growl, he shudders.

"We store no cures."

Right, because a cure for their toxin is like a weapon against them. I expected as much.

I need to get Mona back to the Zarzenius. Or, at least, to Atar. I can't let her suffer like this!

But even as I force the Darzel to continue forward, leading us through the narrow paths till a ship stands before us, I know it's more than that.

Mona's suffering splits me apart. It's true that I can't let her suffer like this…but more so, I can't let her go.

Not like this.

Not ever.

28

Mona

My blood is on fire.

What started as a sharp ache in my chest quickly spread throughout my being and is slowly consuming me.

I'm in shock. I can tell from the way my body convulses, desperate to regain control and rid itself of the threat, but unable to do so.

Am I...am I going to die like this?

I'm dimly aware that Bhihan is rushing into a ship. A Darzel one judging from the familiarity of it. I'm also aware he's shouting at someone, or something. But I can't find the strength to care.

I just want this pain to stop. I want to quell this fire that is eating me from the inside out.

Like a monster clawing beneath my skin, I want to rip through my chest just to pull out the pain.

The ship shudders and jerks as Bhihan sets me on the floor on the bridge, shouting some commands as he hurries to the control panel.

We're leaving this place?

I'm happy for him.

He will be free and not stuck here anymore because of me. This nightmare will end.

And as for me…maybe I was destined to die in this place from the start. No amount of intervention has changed the inevitable.

I'm only sorry I almost brought him down with me.

The ship shudders again, the distinct sound of the engines coming online rushing through the pain clouding my senses as gravity shifts and we move.

He's piloting the ship.

He's got it to listen to him.

My head feels like a log when I try to turn it and it falls like a boulder when I manage the feat.

Through blurred vision, the form of a Darzel restrained on the floor meets my gaze.

He's kidnapped one of them. Probably so he can navigate the ship.

Smart. Brave.

But I already knew all this about him.

He is the most honorable male I have ever met. I'm only sorry my time's running out. I'd have liked to give us a shot. To be his mate. To see if, *for once*, my destiny included something apart from pain and uncertainty. Wariness and ruin.

For a moment, the pain ebbs and my consciousness planes out into a state of calm. I see Bhihan rushing back to me in slow motion and I wonder why he is moving so strangely.

I try to smile at him, but I'm not sure my lips even move. And then, when his fingers brush over my skin, his golden eyes like wide pits in his face as he shouts something at me—my name—everything comes rushing back at once.

My back arches as the pain surges within me and Bhihan grips me, lifting me as he hurries down the corridor.

He places me on a raised area before turning and running his hand through his hair. When he roars is when I realize my ears are ringing. I can't hear a thing.

I *am* dying.

And it will be quick.

Isn't it supposed to be cold? I almost want to beg for the cold, to quell this fire that's eating through me.

Bhihan turns back to me and he lifts my hand, gripping it in his.

The distress on his face almost hurts more than the pain ripping through my veins.

"Bhihan," I try to whisper. "It will be okay."

I thought when my time came, I would go down kicking and screaming. I thought I would fight until the end. I didn't expect this…peace.

And as I look up at him…as I see the complete adoration in his eyes as he clings on to me…I know it's because of him.

In this life that has been filled with nothing but chaos and pain, people who used and deceived me, he has been constant since the day I first met him. He has never let me down. Not even once.

"Mona," he groans, "don't leave me."

I want to repeat that it will be okay. That he will be fine living without me, but even with the pain clouding my judgment, I can see that's not the truth.

Bhihan won't be okay.

And for the first time since this peace began to settle in my mind, I falter.

The thought of leaving him alone, suffering because of me, makes my will return.

My body shakes as my consciousness wanes in and out, but I'm ready to fight again.

I'm far too aware what it's like living with a hollow inside your heart and I…I can't leave him like this.

My head lolls as I try to remain awake and my hand tightens in Bhihan's.

"There's a chance I can save you," he whispers. "I can save you from this."

Pain. So much pain. I can't focus.

I hear his words but they make no sense to me.

"If I mark you, Mona…if I give you my life spirit, I may be able to stop this." He grips my hand tighter, pressing his brow against it. "I can save you…by inflicting a curse on you."

"Do it." Weak, I wonder if he hears me, but his eyes pop open and his throat bobs.

I know why he's hesitating. I know his concerns. But I'd rather die because he tried to save me than die like this.

I squeeze his hand as hard as I can and his throat bobs again.

There's pain in his eyes as he jerks his chin to his chest, letting me know he heard me, before he slowly moves forward.

With one large hand, he tilts my head so my neck is bared, and brings his face close.

In some other time, this would have been intimate, a union of two souls.

I *wanted* his bite. I realize that now.

I wanted him to claim me because no one has ever kept their promise and stuck by me before.

I want to experience that. But the moment his fangs pierce my neck, I scream.

Pain shoots from the contact, making my eyes water and only the pressure of his hand keeping me in place keeps me from thrashing to release myself.

It hurts! It hurts so bad.

Like acid filling me from my neck and spreading inside.

Is it supposed to feel like this?

Something's wrong!

Bhihan grunts against me, wrapping his free hand across my torso to not only hold me in place, but to give me some comfort as he whispers apologies against my skin.

Fire and ice. That's what it feels like. Like two elements warring inside me, each vying for control.

"Bhihan!" I scream, clawing at his arms. I just want it to stop.

Tears run down my cheeks as I cry out, and he shudders beside me, his fangs extracting from my flesh as his tongue swipes out and he licks the wound.

"Please forgive me, my mate." He grips me tighter. "Pain is not what I wish to give you." He shudders holding me even closer, almost as if he wants to draw my pain into himself. "You should be surrounded by blooms and soft things. Protected. Sheltered. Given whatever you desire. And I your humble servant."

Oh Bhihan…

My body is being wracked with pain so extreme, the world goes black.

And even in that moment, where my consciousness breaks under the strain, I feel him still. An unyielding rock that I can rely on.

And I want nothing more than to reach out to him.

But the world races into focus before going black again, and like a weight is attached to my legs, I'm pulled down under the current and into the abyss.

But just as I feel the transition taking over, from life onto another plane, something changes within me. Something deep down that ignites something new.

A spark.

And I know, it's not my time to go yet.

29

Bhihan

As I sit on the floor, back against the cool gray wall, I hold my mate in my arms.

Mona is unmoving. Hardly breathing. Her pulse so weak, I wonder if I am imagining it. And as I sit here, tremors go through me as I wonder what the future holds. All I can do is grip her close to me.

Off, somewhere in the ship, the Darzel I restrained next to the control panel shouts in distress, cursing me and my lineage.

What he doesn't know is that his curses mean nothing to a male destined to kill his mate.

But Mona is resting, or at least, her body is forced to. She is no longer screaming, her body convulsing with pain it cannot control.

The moment I injected her with my life spirit, I knew her reaction might have been extreme. But not to the point that it was.

It took everything within me to not extract my fangs before I filled her veins with my bond. Hearing her scream my name, begging for me to stop, was the hardest thing I have ever had to live through.

Not even in the early days of my existence, when Atar raged great wars and I was on the frontline, was I shattered like I am now.

I am unable to move from this spot, to leave my mate here while I go tend to other things. I can't move. I can't let her go.

And so I sit. I keep her close. I give her my warmth. And I pray to the ancients that she will open her eyes.

I don't know what is happening within her, whether injecting her with life spirit is removing the toxin, or if she is simply in a state of living death.

I've been exposed to the Darzel toxin on so many occasions, I can only hope the antibodies present in my life spirit can save her.

Save her...but give her another burden.

But I won't think about that now. Of Mona attempting to end her life, to rip herself apart all because my life spirit is like fire in her veins.

I cannot bear the thought.

So I will focus on now.

On the fact that she *is* breathing, though barely. And that her life organ still beats. She is still here. She has not gone yet.

30

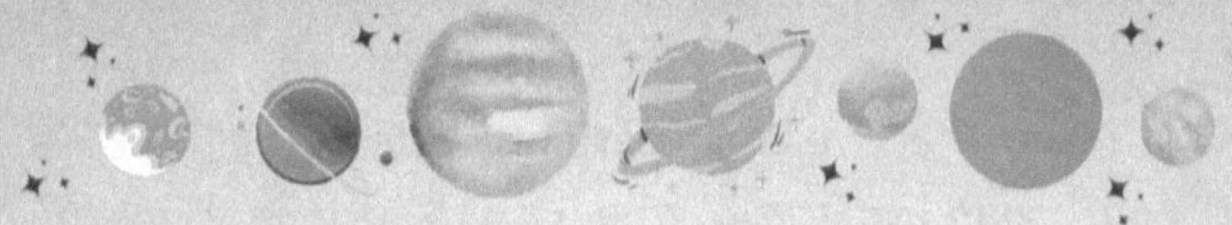

Mona

Light reaches my eyes and I squint, staring at the blurred outline of *something*.

"*Uhh,*" I groan as I try to lift my head.

It feels tight and heavy, heavy enough for my neck to ache as I try to lift it.

And I don't get far.

I only manage to lift it an inch, more blurry objects coming into view, before gentle hands push my head back to the floor.

No, not the floor.

I'm not on the floor.

Whatever I'm on is soft. Not hard. And Bhihan...

"Bhihan?" That croak that leaves my lips sounds nothing like my usual voice. My throat is like a parched desert in need of rain.

"Your mate has not returned to his quarters since he brought you here." The female that speaks has a soothing voice that relaxes me even when it shouldn't. "He's not far, but has been restricted from your presence for our safety. We will let him know you have awakened."

Restricted? Have they done something to him? And who is this? Where am I?

Something appears before my face. I can't make it out, but it beeps before it's moved down the rest of my body.

"It appears the Darzel toxin has reduced below critical levels," the woman says.

"Wh-where am I? Wh-why can't I see anything?" I hate the way my voice cracks and the slight tremor in it.

"You are at the Royal Medical Center."

Huh?

"It is not often that we treat patients outside of the royal bloodline...but your mate...*insisted*. The crown prince himself granted access."

I can't see her face, but the way she says it, as if that is something that also does not usually happen, makes me uneasy.

So... I survived. And Bhihan took me to his planet. He made sure I lived.

Where is he? I want to see him. I *need* to see him.

The urge to get off this bed and find him, be with him is so strong, I try to move only to be pressed back down by who I assume is a nurse.

"You are not yet fit for movement."

But I *need* to see him. Something deep inside me quivers and grows warm, fluttering in the center of my chest so hard that I lift a weak arm to the spot.

It almost feels like there's something *alive* underneath my skin and I clutch my chest.

I'm no longer half-naked. Dressed in some sort of soft material that feels more expensive than anything I've ever worn before. The fabric folds in my fist as I grip my chest, partial anxiety rising.

What *is* this feeling?

As if a flexible cord, filled with biomaterial that's connected somewhere deep inside me, is tugging, pulling against something else outside of myself.

Anxiety transforms into fear as sudden alarm spreads from the other end of the cord and races through my being. But it's almost as if that feeling isn't my own.

Bhihan…

I need Bhihan!

Even as I think about him, I can sense his presence coming straight through that cord. And then I remember. I remember it all. His words before he sunk his fangs into my neck.

Of what he'd said before to me while we'd been stuck in the cell.

Bhihan bit me. He fought for me, and then he claimed me.

This indescribable feeling can be none other than one thing.

This is the bond.

Tears blur my already shaky vision when the door flies open.

I don't need to see him to know he is there. *I can feel him.* Every cell within me seems to rejoice and grow warm the closer he gets.

There's a ruckus behind him, shouts of distress and alarm as he storms into the room and when his hands cup my face, I can only sob with relief.

"Bhihan…"

"Thank the gods."

I don't need to see it in his face, I can hear it clearly. The utter relief at seeing me awake.

"You were worried about me," I whisper.

"More than anything."

Another sob racks through me and Bhihan's hands tremble against my cheeks. "You're still in pain."

I shake my head but it causes little sharp pains to shoot through my skull, making me wince despite the brave face I'm trying to put on.

"You must sedate her once more," Bhihan growls. "She must not feel discomfort. She must not endure the pain."

His voice sounds different. Rough. almost like he's snarling and his skin against my cheeks heats as the seconds tick by. But I don't want him to let me go.

"I can assure you, *oli*, that your mate's aches are not at the level they were before. She has stepped back from the point of no return."

A growl rumbles in the room and when the nurse gasps, I think there's an animal somewhere close. Something large and dangerous.

But there's rage mixed in with fear that's emanating from the bond in my chest, and I realize, the beast that's growling is him. My mate.

Bhihan.

I lift my hand, tracing it up his chest and the threatening rumbling suddenly stops. The room is silent as my fingers brush up his neck and over his lips, so close to his fangs, I feel the sharp tip of one.

Bhihan licks his lips, a whimper going through the large male as his tongue brushes against my finger.

His outline is still blurry but I recognize he's watching me intently anyway.

"Mona?"

"Bhihan," I whisper, "I survived."

A breath shudders from his chest and he strokes my jaw.

The bond thrums between us, filling me with warmth.

This feeling…is like being filled with pure, unfiltered love. Feeling him here, his presence always with me, I wonder what had made me afraid of this before.

"Have you completed the tests?" he asks.

Tests? Which tests?

"Yes, *oli*. Your mate's lifeblood…"

Her pause makes me tilt my head her way, and across the bond, coming from Bhihan is a fear that had been lingering there, carefully hidden, from the start.

"…it still holds low levels of the Darzel toxin. We can remove it from her completely. However…"

However what?

Her pause once more makes more fear come through the bond and I wonder what's causing her to hesitate.

"Your…condition. Your *curse*…"

Is it just me, or did she say that with a side of disgust unnecessarily served.

It hits me then, that Bhihan has had to live like this, on his world, with people who refer to something he can't control with such revulsion…*all the time*.

My heart aches and right along with it is a feeling of rage so strong I probably would have punched her if I could.

This is no different from how I've been treated back on my home planet.

Loathed.

And for what?

Of all the people I've ever met, Bhihan is the least to deserve that.

I open my mouth to berate her when her next words have me pausing.

"The tests have returned and what we theorized is true. The effect of your life spirit…" she pauses, making us wait "is counteracted by the Darzel toxin."

What?

"As long as your mate is fed the toxin, she will not suffer the fate of the females in your line."

I feel Bhihan freeze.

Silence descends in the room apart from soft beeps from what I assume to be the medical equipment.

"You want me to infest her being with the same thing that almost took her away from me?" Bhihan growls. "To bring her pain and to the brink of death over and over again just so I can have her as my mate?"

The woman is unbelievably calm with what sounds like a big angry male snarling in her face. "With the right dosage, she will feel no pain."

"I cannot risk it."

"If you don't, your life spirit will revert from *healing*…to *destroying*…and you will lose your mate."

"Yes." The word is almost a whisper, but I hear it anyway and the bond between us pulses and pulls.

I don't want to lose him. Not yet. And I realize now, I was never ready to.

"I will have her reject this bond. Go to the priests, the shamans, whatever it takes. She will live. Even if I must keep my distance and watch her from afar. She will live."

My heart breaks and the bond pulses, tugging on his end. I want to pull him closer. I want to feel his arms around me

But he stands rigid. Unmoving.

I wish I could see his face. See what thoughts his eyes reveal.

But I don't need to. The bond tells me everything. And all I can feel is that his heart is breaking just as mine. Shattering to pieces.

His words, the bravado, it's all an act. A lie.

Bhihan wants me just as badly as I want him and for the first time in my life, this is something I don't want to let go.

"I'll do it." I turn my head in the direction of the nurse, my blurred vision settling on her. "I'll take the toxin. We'll fight this thing."

"Mona…"

"Sign me up." The tremor in my voice makes me swallow hard. "Sign me up. I'll do it."

Bhihan grips my hand tighter. "Mona, it's a risk that—"

"That I am willing to take."

He stares at me for a few moments, before he bends, leaning close. "Why…Why put yourself in such danger?"

Well, that's easy to answer.

I tilt my head up to him. "For you. You fought for me, Bhihan. Now it's my turn to fight for you."

31

Bhihan

I shouldn't feel such pride as I walk through the medical center with my mate. I shouldn't feel like a king who's just won the greatest conquest.

But I do.

I feel like the luckiest male alive.

Mona, *my mate*, keeps my hand in hers even as I walk next to the floating bed that moves alongside us as we leave the building.

Despite the attention we receive, she does not let me go. She holds me as if I am a male worthy of her matehood…

I'm not afraid of many things…but Mona's acceptance is something that I'm almost too afraid to conceive.

All the Atari medics that pass us in the halls, all that now know of my…condition…look at me through eyes that don't hide their fear, nor their disgust.

But Mona…

I know she can't see me well. Her vision will return in a few cycles. But even though she can't gaze upon me properly, the complete warmth in her eyes when she turns my way sends delicious chills down my spine from a source deep within me.

This female was out of her mind when she hopped into the void and caught my attention. But I am never more joyous for her wild antics than I am now. And I wonder, would I have ever found her had she not arrived in my life the way she did?

Would I have spent eons alone on the Zarzenius, hiding from the very thing that's giving my life purpose now?

"I can take it from here." The attendant who was escorting us through the medical center bows slightly before shuffling away and I grasp the floating bed, directing it to the hover car waiting in the bay.

"Bhihan?" Mona's husky voice. The way she says my name. A delicious shiver goes down my spine. "Are we alone now?"

Yes. Finally. "Just the two of us."

I have waited, pacing the halls of that medical center, for days while they worked to pump the toxin from her veins. It was a hell I don't want to live in ever again.

"Now, I will take you home."

Home.

A place I haven't seen in many moons. But the word has new meaning now that Mona is here.

"So this is your planet?" She turns her head, tilting it to the skies as she tries to take in the view and I wish her vision was fully healed. But she will have many other opportunities to see Atar. After all, this is her new home. Her new life.

"It's beautiful," she whispers. "I wish I could see it better."

"And you will, my mate."

Mona smiles, gripping my hand tighter as I lock the bed in place. Speaking to the artificial intelligence, I tell it to take us home, and as the door closes and we move through the transport tubes, Mona simply stares through the window, her eyes settled on the movement and the bright lights reflecting off the towers.

For the first time since I met her, there is calm. Her features are relaxed and despite what she just went through, despite the agony that must have even tortured her soul, she...smiles.

"I'm...happy." She finally whispers, squeezing my hand once more. "This is nice."

I move closer, lifting a hand to her brow to move away one of her braids just so I have nothing obstructing her beautiful face. I could sit here, staring at her for many moons.

My mate is *perfection*.

Inhaling deeply is not enough.

I want to press my face into her skin and soak her in. I want her scent all over me, and mine on her. I want her arousal as a constant scent on my lips, tormenting me every waking moment until I can sate my need by delving deep within her folds.

"Bhihan," she whimpers, pulling me closer, and I have no choice but to lean over her awkwardly, bracing my arms against the sides of the bedding so I don't crush her.

"Are you in pain?" Concerns halts every other feeling within me.

"Yes," she whimpers, but when I try to ease upright so I can check the list of medications, she grips on to my arm tighter.

"I..." she begins. She turns her head in my direction, her unfocused gaze moving with slight uncertainty. "It's not that type of pain."

I...don't understand.

"It's here." She lifts her hand, the thin robes the medics dressed her in swaying as she grips her chest. "It's warm. Hot. And I...it's spreading outward. I can feel it in my..."

She swallows hard but I know now what she is referring to.

These past few cycles, while she battled the toxin and fought to return to me, the bond between us grew. I could feel her fear, her pain, her distress. I could feel her hope and her regrets.

I could feel everything. And it was the sensation of those regrets that made this all the more torturous.

But Mona can also feel the bond. She will be feeling every sensation coming from me, and at awareness of that, I close my mind off.

It was easy to ignore the ache of the bond when Mona was fighting for her life. But now, now that she has passed that critical stage, it seems the bond has awakened not only its ability for sensation relay... but the burning need it creates for us to rut until we create a new being.

Mona grips me tighter, her chest heaving and she tries to control the sudden urge arising within her.

"Bhihan?" she murmurs, uncertainty in her tone.

I swallow hard. She is not ready for this.

She has hardly accepted me as her mate for the bond to be forcing us to rut. And so soon after she has faced such difficulty.

"Bhihan." More uncertainty in her voice now. And desperation.

I groan. I should have asked the medic for a rut suppressant.

They are frowned upon, but what other choice do I have? I never expected Mona to be feeling the urge.

I can control myself. I would never take from her what she's unwilling to give. And thought of her rejecting me keeps me in my place.

But Mona is not Atari. She doesn't know how to control the undeniable pull of the bond.

The urge to seal the deal, for me to sink into her, is like a call that's drawing me closer even though she hasn't uttered the words.

"It hurts," she whimpers, her fingers finding their way to the back of my neck where that sensitive spot lies. I almost growl in pleasure. "I need you."

I freeze.

Did she just say…

"Please Bhihan, I need you," Mona says again. "Like the first time when I wanted you, but this is different. I *need* you now."

Her words are beautiful, even though they are simply the truth. She needs me, not because she wants my comfort, but because she is my mate and only I can sate that burning need spreading through her being.

"We will arrive at my lodging—"

"No. I can't wait. I need you now."

I hesitate again.

Our first time joining should be a celebration. I want to take her in a place where she will feel safe. Secure. Not in the hover car where—

"I know what you're thinking," she whispers. "I can feel it." Easing upward she comes so close to me that her breath brushes against my lips.

"I don't want anything else. All I want is you right now, Bhihan. Will you deny me?"

A growl rumbles deep in my chest at the thought.

How could I ever?

32

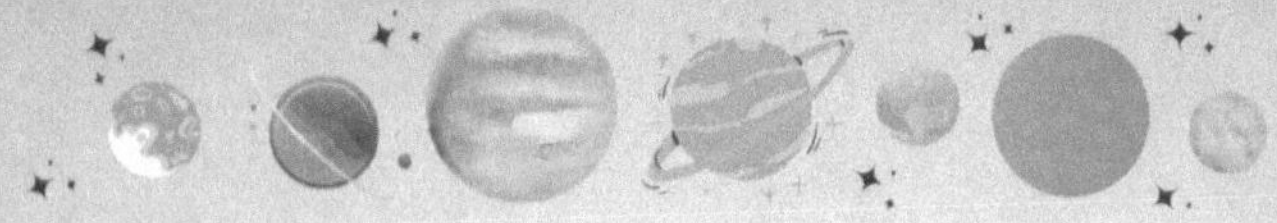

Mona

Bhihan's growl is all I hear before his mouth crashes against mine. His kiss is so gentle, yet so demanding. As if he's a dangerous animal that has been watching his prey for far too long and now he has the chance to have it all, yet he's too afraid to make that move. For once he does, his prey will be no more.

I whimper against his lips, the ache in my head fading away as soon as his skin touches mine. Bhihan kisses me as if he will lose me soon. As if after this moment, I will disappear into dust, and for the first time in my life, I feel wanted. Needed.

This male needs me just as much as I desperately need him.

I want to tell him that I'm not going anywhere. That this feels like forever, but his lips don't slip from mine.

A moan escapes me when I feel him climb on top of the floating bed. It doesn't sway, even though I can feel his weight pressing the fibers in.

Every corded muscle in his chest seems to be beckoning me, and when my fingers skate over his pecs, Bhihan growls, rumbling a deep sound into my mouth that makes me melt. Instant moisture seeps from my center and another whimper releases from me.

I've never wanted a male the way I want Bhihan. Never before has my body heated and called for another's touch the way it is now. And I finally understand why.

Before, I'd thought it was because of my demons. That the darkness followed me and I didn't deserve anything good. That my place on New Earth was penance for some sin I committed in my past life.

That I didn't deserve it all.

But now I know the truth.

The reason nobody else ever mattered before, was because they weren't meant to. Fate intended someone special for me. And here he is, kissing me as if there is no tomorrow.

Bhihan growls, a shudder going through his shoulders when I match his kiss, my tongue swiping against his, need pooling in my belly.

I spread my leg, forcing him to settle against me, and just the feel of his thick frame makes me clench.

"You are unwell. Hurt. In pain. We shouldn't—"

Breaking the kiss, I can tell he's about to pull away. Because he's chivalrous. Honorable.

But I don't want chivalry right now.

I want a man to rip these fairy robes off and fuck me like I'm his whore. *My* man. I want to hurt in the best way, and only he can give that to me.

"Don't stop," I whisper, my naturally husky voice taking on a tone that drips with the need that's threatening to take me over. "Don't you dare stop."

I can't see him well, and I wish I could. But it doesn't matter. I have something better. I can *feel* him.

And he's everything I ever wanted.

Bhihan's end of the cord that binds us is overflowing with care, protection, love, and warmth.

"I've lived all my life never feeling anything like this." I press a hand against his chest and his muscles ripple at my touch. "All my life I've lived feeling like I was a mistake." Taking his tunic into my fist, I pull him closer once more, until I feel his lips brush against mine once more.

"I want to feel you, Bhihan. Let me feel you."

He doesn't resist.

The urge is so great that when he lifts the robes, spreading them so I am bare before him, I am practically tingling.

Bhihan growls at the sight of me, and for a moment, I think he doesn't like what he sees. That's before a surge of lust goes through the bond so hard, that my center quivers, need seeping to moisten the robes beneath me.

He wants me more than he wants air itself and that thought makes my body sing.

I'm aware he shuffles, his lips slipping across mine as he shrugs out of his clothes, and when his hot skin presses into me, it's heaven filled with bliss.

Reaching between us, the hard length of his cock is like a second furnace that makes me quiver.

I don't want to wait, I need him now, and when I guide him to me, sliding him through my slick folds, the shudder and resulting moan that comes from my mate is the greatest gift.

He's just as tortured as I am. Just as broken. Just as deserving.

His flared head sends ripples through my clit as his heat connects with mine and Bhihan dips his head to my neck, his hot breaths brushing over my skin as he shudders with my movement.

"We're in a hover car," he murmurs, tongue flicking out to lick my neck.

"Can people see us?"

"If they look."

"Does that bother you?"

"We are mates." He pauses. "I only care what you think."

For a moment, I hesitate but realize quickly that I don't care. I don't care if others catch glimpses of Bhihan claiming me as we speed down this superhighway. I don't care if others see this celebration between our beings.

I want to shout it from the rooftops. He is mine and I am his. And just when I've tortured myself enough, his cock twitching against my folds as traces of our arousal meld, Bhihan shifts so he is lined up with my entrance.

My eyes flutter open then as his hand moves up to cup my jaw.

"My Mona," he growls before he eases forward.

Despite my efforts to relax, I stiffen, the sensation of his size against my small opening making me pause. He's so big, all I can think of is that maybe he won't fit, but as he eases forward some more, that flared head of his bends and molds as he pushes into me.

My back presses into the bedding as I bite my bottom lip, a moan escaping from my mouth even though I'm holding my breath.

The pain/pleasure is almost too much as Bhihan grips my bum, spreading me for him as he eases forward some more, before pulling back.

His rhythm is one I adjust to as he stretches me beyond how much I imagined he would, and when his hips begin to piston, leaving no space between us, I can only whimper his name as sensations I never thought I'd ever feel come crashing through me.

Bhihan fucks me like he will never get enough. He whispers words I don't know, words in Atari that sound like he's speaking to the gods. But even though I don't understand his words, I get the meaning straight from the bond.

They're words of thanks and praise.

Bhihan is telling me that he will never be able to live without me. And I...

I know I will never be able to leave his side.

EPILOGUE

Mona

"Bhihan?"

The long gown I wear sways in the slight breeze coming through the window as I turn away from the view of the Atari city.

Here in our house, where the sun shines and flowers bloom, life is the complete opposite of what it was back on New Earth.

My new leg taps slightly on the decorated flooring as I walk through the house, the only sound apart from my own breathing in my ears.

"Bhihan?"

He does this. Disappears for some time and when I finally find him, he's doing something to his house that he says is completely necessary.

Last time it was installing all sorts of rails in the two upstairs bathrooms because, and I quote, "he would die if his mate ever slipped and fell because she didn't have something to hold on to." Or that time he had deliveries coming all day, stocking the kitchen, because god forbid "his mate ever have hunger pains when he's not around and there's no food for her to consume."

Yesterday, I woke to see a crew of workmen all around the grounds.

According to one, the master was "renovating the entire garden with blooms of bright and rare flowers because his mate deserved a beautiful space."

He has been working non-stop, even though I've told him I don't need all these things. Yet, he insists.

And…as time has passed, I've realized it's not that I don't need these things. It's that I've convinced myself I could do without. All those years fending for myself, it's hard adjusting to this. It's hard allowing someone else to take care of me.

Yet, there's also something else.

The way Bhihan has been working hard, as if he wants to give me no excuse to say he's a bad mate. As if he almost believes this is temporary, and he's doing everything in his power to make me happy.

To make me stay.

As I walk to the other end of the large house, much bigger than any place I've ever lived in before, I can't help but feel content.

Atar is…beautiful. Like some sort of paradise, and sometimes I wonder if I've been dreaming.

The house itself *is* like a dream. Pristine with white walls that look like they're made of marble, set with a view of the city itself.

Climbing onto the lift that takes me to the upper level of the house, I automatically lean on the wall to take pressure off my leg. Habit. Because I no longer need to do that. My new leg feels almost as real as my biological one.

As the lift comes to a halt and I step off it, I perk my ears for any sound.

I almost miss it, but the trickling of water in the bath reaches my ear.

Oh, Bhihan…

I now know why he is so silent.

He always gets like that when he's completely focused on this task and when I walk into the washroom, there he is kneeling before the bath, a tray with syringes balanced along its edge as he reaches in and checks the temperature of the water.

I can tell it's warm from the steam that emanates, filling the room, and I can't help but smile.

"Bhihan," I whisper.

His ears twitch as he turns and looks at me, his gaze becoming hungry the moment his eyes land on me. It's a look I can never get enough of.

"You didn't have to," I whisper.

He always does this now. Sets out the syringes with the fabricated Darzel toxin with precision. Each dose not one milliliter more than it should be. And a hot bath to soothe my bones as my body rejects the toxin and my life spirit takes on the fight.

We do it every week and it's my third dose now. Every time, it gets easier.

As I move toward him, he pulls me into his arms, settling on the floor as I straddle him.

"Join me this time?"

Strands from his hair fall over his face as he tilts his head to look at me and beneath that warmth, that consuming fire of love and need, I see his hesitation.

The same hesitation that lingers like a shadow between us.

A breath releases through his nose as he tilts forward, capturing my lips in his. His kiss is sweet, slow, and leaves me wanting more when he finally pulls away.

"Come now, my mate. Let us do this."

He's tense. I can feel it in his muscles. And when I make no effort to move off him, his brows furrow a little.

Taking my face between his hands, he rests his forehead against mine. Golden eyes close as he speaks to me.

"I know you may not want to. I'm sorry you have to endure this for the rest of your life." A breath shudders from him. "I know you didn't choose any of this, and I promise you, I will do everything in my power to ensure you don't spend the other parts of your days in such agony and pain."

"Oh, Bhihan," I grasp his hands and push away from him so I can look at him properly. His eyes pop open the moment I do and the pain lingering there comes through the bond like an open wound. "Is that why you've been working so hard? To make me happy?"

The fact he doesn't answer tells me everything I'd already assumed.

"Do you think I will change my mind and leave or something?"

I'm not going to lie. Despite that I know where it's coming from, a part of me is pissed he's even thinking that.

Grasping his tunic at the collar, surprise echoes in his eyes as I pull him forward, close enough that my lips brush against his as I speak.

"I chose you, you fool. I don't want anyone else. I never will. And I'm not going anywhere."

His throat moves as he swallows hard and between us, the bond thrums like a dog wagging its tail.

"I wasn't thrown into this without choices. I'm here because I want to be and because…"

The words come to my lips and render me speechless. As my lips part, Bhihan's gaze falls to them and he watches them, looking like he's caught between the temptation of pulling them into his mouth and waiting to hear what I have to say.

"I love you, Bhihan."

Saying the words is like lifting something from my shoulders that I didn't know I'd been carrying. And through the bond, I feel a deep, resounding thump as if Bhihan's heart swelled a thousand times in that one second.

"You love me…"

"I do." Tears aren't in my eyes, right? Because I don't want to cry. Right?

But when Bhihan lifts a finger and wipes a tear away, another one escapes. "I love you so much."

"Oh, my ari," he says, pulling me into him. "My ari."

The word warms me from head to toe.

The Atari word for "mate" means much more than simply "one who was fated to me."

I can feel what it means through the bond.

It means a soulmate that is destined to complete me, a partner that will stand by my side through thick and thin. Bhihan is my ari, and as he holds me close to his chest, I know that I have found my other half.

It's like the world around me fades away, and all that matters is the warmth of Bhihan's embrace.

"The Atari don't use the word 'love' as you do, my ari," he says.

"But know you are my everything. That I would face wars for you, fight for you against countless enemies. That I would travel to the very ends of the universe and back if it meant that I could find you and keep you safe. If it meant that I could keep you happy, I would bring the stars down from the heavens for you. If it meant that I could show my love, I'd paint the city red for you. I would craft sculptures and buildings in your name, and give you the world if you simply ask for it."

He kisses me softly on the forehead, his eyes filled with such love and devotion that I feel my heart swell with emotion. "You are my ari, Mona. Mine. My mate. You are my queen."

I grip him tighter. His words mean more to me than he will ever know.

"And you, Bhihan…you are my king."

AFTERWORD

♥ This concludes Fighting for His Mate ♥

Hey there!
I hope you enjoyed Mona and Bhihan's story.
I knew these two would be a great match from the moment I thought
of Mona's character. She was based off many of the strong females I
had in my life growing up, and her quick wit and spunk make me
think of her as a person I'd love to have as a friend.
I have to admit, Bhihan surprised me. He's this tough, no-nonsense
warrior, but underneath it all, he's got a such a soft heart.
I just wanted to thank you for taking the time to read this book. I had
so much fun writing it, and I hope it brings you joy.

Thank you so much for reading and as always, lots of love and many
blessings!

♥ A.G.

Scan the QR code below if you want to ☞ Join my mailing list, ☞ Find
me on Facebook , or ☞ Join my Patreon (exclusive access NSFW character art, ARCs, sneak peeks, and more!)

Guarding His Mate

ALSO BY AGWILDE

Xul: Captured by Aliens Book One

Athena wakes up in hell.

Well…it's an alien slave ship, but it might as well be hell because she only has three choices.

Mate. Become a sex slave. Or be killed.

Great options.

Desperate for freedom, a chance for survival is presented in the handsome rogue alien called Xul.

But Xul is caught up in problems of his own and a mission he cannot afford to let fail—one that could be easily compromised if he dared open his heart.

That doesn't leave her with many options and it doesn't help that she finds him utterly frustrating...

...and strong, hot, irresistible…

She shouldn't really be thinking about him like that. Should she?

Other books in the series: Crex, Yce, Kyris, Kyro

———

Riv's Sanctuary: Riv's Sanctuary Book One

Abducted from Earth over a year ago, Lauren spent most of that time getting accustomed to her new life as one of the "animals" in an alien zoo.

When she's sold by the zookeeper, her life takes a turn she wasn't expecting. She has no idea where she'll end up till she's brought to a sanctuary owned by a tall blue hunk of an alien called Riv.

Riv's life is quiet and peaceful in a place as far away from civilization as he can manage. So when an annoying chatterbox of a human ends up on his doorstep, he's less than pleased. The human disrupts his life and his solitude and he can't wait to get rid of her.

He's not interested in helping her, and he's definitely not interested in love.

Except…she's managed to wheedle her way in and suddenly those barriers around his heart don't seem so strong anymore.

He has two options: Let her go.

Or let her in.

Other books in the series: Sohut's Protection, Ka'Cit's Haven

———

Ajos: The Restitution Book One

She didn't move to the big city just to be kidnapped by aliens.

That wasn't even possible...

Right?

WRONG.

When Kerena wakes up, she's not on Earth anymore.

Heck, she's not even in the same galaxy, and the face hovering so close she can make out every detail? That face is definitely...not...human.

But before she can really figure out what's going on, Kerena realizes she's caught in the middle of a war—one she was thrust into as soon as she was ripped from Earth.

She's surrounded by aliens in a rebellion, but there's one—the one with the strange golden eyes, minty-teal skin, and rippling muscles—that holds her attention.

His presence is magnetic and his heated gaze makes something stir deep within her.

He's battling something that has nothing to do with the war and his warning that she should stay away does not go unheeded.

He's a dangerous rebel fighter. She gets that. So...why is he still hovering so close? And why is he growling at everyone that so much as looks in her direction?

Most of all, why does he keep looking at her like she belongs to ... HIM?

Other books in the series: V'Alen

——

Arrival: Captured Earth Book One

ADIRA

The machines came, and they trampled us all.

I have nothing left. No family. No friends. No home.

They harvest us. They breed us. They feed from us…

There is no hope…Not until one fateful moment when my eyes open and I see something streaking across the skies.

What appears is like a demon before my eyes…

But can they be worse than the evil already upon us?

I will just have to wait and see.

FER'RO

Sailing across the stars for what feels like eons…we have followed our enemy to a little blue planet.

We had wanted to arrive before them…now I think we may be too late.

But when we kill the first Scrit and I see the being drowning within its depths, I know I have to save it.

And *it*…turns out to be a *her*. **A female.**

This planet has hope yet. I will save her and her kind.

…Little do I know…she's the one who ends up saving me instead.

Dark. Steamy. Gritty. A thrilling romance intertwined in a plot that will give you chills.

Other books in the series: Base Zero, Cataclysm, War

——

Claiming His Mate
Fated Mates of the Atari

When I get a once-in-a-lifetime chance to go on a luxury space cruise, I jump at it.
This cruise is the beginning of something amazing, and nothing is going to stop me from going.
But when things go wrong shortly after departure, it's clear I have made a mistake.
Suddenly thrown into a world where I have no way of defending myself, the last thing I expect is an Atari warrior coming to my rescue.
This cruise has been full of surprises…but the Atari is the biggest one of all.
He's tall, growly, possessive, and he sends my pulse into overdrive with just the slightest look.
Why the heck is my body reacting this way to this stranger?
And did he just declare that I am his mate?

Other books in the series: Craving His Mate, Fighting for His Mate, Guarding His Mate

——

Scan the QR code to view all books

ABOUT THE AUTHOR

A. G. Wilde is an avid reader, a gamer, a lover of all things space, alien, and sci-fi.

She is addicted to intense romance, irresistible heroes, and deliciously naughty things.

❋☆☼☆❋

patreon.com/agwilde
facebook.com/agwilde
twitter.com/authoragwilde
instagram.com/authoragwilde
amazon.com/author/agwilde